MW01171165

LORD ALEXANDER THE

MAFIA VAMPIRE

AN UNEXPECTED SUMMONING BY THE VAMPIRE GOD VINCENT

Lord Alexander brutally and sadistically murdered a gender bender vampire and her dwarf husband. Princess Tiffanie and Saul grew infuriated over their unnatural deaths by the hand of Lord Alexander. The ghosts demanded a meeting with the King of New Orleans. The King's butler William greeted them and said, "Lord Alexander is busy, and he tasked me to seal you away in a soul jar." William the dwarf pulled out a black soul jar and said the magical phrase, "Woogedy Boogedy Boo, your soul no longer belongs to you." Princess and Saul were swiftly sealed away by William in the black soul jar. The gender bender fanger and dwarf would not shut the fuck up and bitched as their ghostly bodies were sucked deep inside the soul jar.

An hour later the King arrived at the Esplanade Mansion and declared the old-world phrase "The White People" as invalid as it did not include vampires of other races. Lord Alexander proclaimed vampires were now the Silver People due to their silver auras and platinum colored vampire wings. The Gold People was a title reserved for the only Vampire God in existence due to having the only golden aura and massive gold vampire wings. There was also a secret vampire handshake the King learned from the Vampire God. The secret vampire handshake is distinct in that you place your index and middle finger on the vampire's wrist to check for a pulse. No pulse equals an authentic vampire and a genuine immortal that is undead. A high-speed pulse meant a crackhead goth wannabe that got a hold of the wrong shit and told it to play a vampire.

The Vampire God telepathically summoned the King to Jackson Square, at the stroke of midnight. Lord Alexander ran the new vampire code words by Vampire God Vincent, and he seemed delighted at his genius way of thinking. Vampire God Vincent proclaimed, "I have been alive since before the life of Christ and I had thousands of years to come up with something that catchy!" Lord

Alexander told the Vampire God Vincent

about his butler sealing away the two

ghosts. Vampire God Vincent said,

"Sometimes you just need to seal a

motherfucker! You put the laughter in

manslaughter for sure. That degenerate

gender bending vampire Tiffanie and its

queer lover had it coming for far too

long." The two vampires sat at Big Gay

Salazar's fortune teller setup and smoked

their brains out with the finest of herb.

Vampire God Vincent told Lord

Alexander the new code words would be honored for future vampire generations.

Lord Alexander left the Vampire God to visit his favorite bar, The Boozy and Floozy Witch found on Bourbon and Toulouse Street. It was December 25, 2022, and a little past one in the morning. Big Gay Salazar took a huge toke and waved as Lord Alexander strolled over to the vampire bar. The five ginger vampire babes were waiting for Lord Alexander and bought the King a goblet filled with the infamous Midnight Potion drink mixed with the blood of Russian children and their tears. Vampires can only consume alcohol, tears or blood and not human food. Vampires like humans can get white girl wasted on alcohol and do stupid shit. Lord Alexander drank five or six golden goblets of Midnight Potion served by the boozy and floozy witch, Zarah Elizabeth Jackson. Lord Alexander got so drunk on the juices of life that he paid for the entire bar's tab four times over with vampire gold.

Lord Alexander in his intoxicated state decided to stretch out his silver wings and flew over to Café Du Monde hidden in City Park. On the way there he spotted Lord Baar's blacked out Ford Explorer. Lord Alexander drunk and pissed off at the world fell like Satan to the Earth. He decided in his drunkard state of mind to trash Lord Baar's explorer. Lord

Alexander scooped up the over-powered SUV and threw it into the Big Lake. Lord Alexander was not satisfied with only water damage and dove in after the Explorer. He decided to throw the blacked-out vehicle into an industrial vehicle incinerator instead. Lord Alexander was angry at Lord Baar for making him a vampire and ruining his life with the curse of immortality.

Lord Alexander became such a lecherous, whoremongering drunkard. He drank enough that he bought everyone at Café Du Monde enough beignets to kill 100s of diabetics. Lord Alexander spotted three blonde dwarfs and asked, "Do your parents know where you are at tonight?" The dwarves replied in unison, "You may be the Vampire King of New Orleans, but short dwarf jokes are where we draw the goddamn line!" The three angry dwarfs attacked the King and he laughed and laughed. Lord Alexander dodged every punch and kick with ease even though he was drunker than five skunks. Lord Alexander told the little bearded devils, "Do you little monsters want to die a gruesome and violent death tonight?" They pulled out a silver chain with spikes on the end and tried to hit the King.

Lord Alexander grabbed all three dwarves by the beard and flew towards the heavens. The dwarves screamed in terror as the King tossed them and caught them in the atmosphere. Lord Alexander danced

endlessly in the sky swinging the dwarfs

around like he was in satanic trance. One

of the little people said, "Lord Alexander,

I heard you are like nine foot tall, or

something put us down you vampire prick!

We are only three foot nothing and stand

no real chance with a vampire fiend of

your caliber. Do you not have any decency

you devil motherfucker you?" Lord

Alexander exclaimed with his booming

voice, "I am the Devil, and I am here to do

the Devil's work! Look into my eyes you

little piss ant! You are staring into the eyes

of Satan!'"

The dwarves continued to scream in agony

as Lord Alexander bit them on their little

necks and siphoned the life out of their

tiny bodies. After the King killed the little

people; he had hurled their bodies into the

bayou to feed Sampson the alligator. The

King in his drunkard old codger state of

mind flew his ass back to the Esplanade

Mansion to sleep off his incredible

intoxication. Around three in the morning Lord Alexander got his vampire drunkard ass out of bed and went proposing marriage to both humans and vampires. Lord Alexander went to Lesley Rubles quarters situated on the second floor of the Esplanade Mansion and tried tirelessly to woo her into marriage. Lesley was unhappy with being awake at such a dreadful hour. Lesley glared at the King until he vomited up the Midnight Potion and stumbled his old honey badger ass back to bed.

Lord Alexander slept off the intoxication in his seventh-floor penthouse for three nights. Zarah Jackson rudely roused the King and she stood at the foot of his bed wearing nothing but pink panties. Lord Alexander said to Zarah, "How on God's green earth did you slip passed the guards and our hyper advanced security system? Drunkard Zarah said, "My methods are simply supernatural. I need your vampire dick deep inside my love box." The King scolded her with a slap to the face and said, "Not now woman I have some top-secret vampire business that supersedes any plans you may have tonight." Zarah gave the King a ferocious uppercut that would make Liu Kang proud. The King's Elite Daytime Guardians arrived and escorted the mad hoe off the property.

Scores of Lord Baar's homeless gay lovers arrived at the Esplanade Mansion seeking refuge from the Louisiana heat. Lord

Alexander was not too happy with uninvited guests. Lord Alexander and the five ginger vampire babes drained their necks and tossed them in the bayou for Sampson the alligator and his children to devour.

Lord Alexander handpicked the Elite Daytime Guardians for daylight protection against all enemies of the vampire crown, both foreign and domestic. These men were the deadliest Marines in the world, and nobody could beat them in hand-to-hand combat. These eight men were part of Project Hercules in the Marine Corps and took hundreds of lives so the enemies could meet their respective gods. Project Hercules was an experimental drug given to Force Recon Marines that gave them superior vision, improved their reflexes, and made them invulnerable to bullets or explosives. Their skin would repair itself after almost any battle wound. So long as the Elite Daytime Guardians did not become decapitated, they were invincible. The Elite Daytime Guardians stole their motto from that 'Mad Dog' Marine Corps General, be polite, be professional, but have a plan to kill everyone you meet.

The leader of the Elite Daytime Guardians was Kreaper. He was average height for a Marine and became bald due to a IED explosion in Afghanistan. Kreaper was barrel-chested, broad shouldered and sported a goatee. Kreaper cussed like a battle-hardened Marine and had a deep thick Texas accent. The leader of the Elite

Daytime Guardians could punch as hard as a newly turned vampire thanks to Project Hercules permanently changing his D.N.A. Out of all the Elite Daytime Guardians, Kreacher was the fastest, strongest, and wisest of them all. Kreacher would wake up the EDGs at 04:00 to go for a ten-mile run every morning. The EDGs routine would be wake up at 03:00 eat a protein and carb rich breakfast and beat the holy fuck out of each other until it was time to go running like nobody's business.

After their morning run the Elite Daytime Guardians would go to their underground shooting range and practice their skills nonstop for four hours every day. They Elite Daytime Guardians got extraordinarily little sleep and did not need it thanks to Project Hercules making their bodies require little rest.

The Elite Daytime Guardians had a strict schedule and finished by 10:00 am to patrol the Esplanade Mansion. The

Mansion was massive in size and had 442

rooms and was seven stories tall

overlooking Bayou St. John. They

travelled in two teams of four and never

travelled together to throw off any

intruders tracking their exact patrol routes.

The Elite Daytime Guardians split into

two teams with one team inside the

Mansion and the other outside. Teams

Alpha and Omega rotated inside and

outside the Esplanade Mansion so they

would have multiple perspectives. Both Teams wore computerized camouflage uniforms that automatically adapted to any landscape or environment. The Elite Daytime Guardians were experts in light-footed walking, and most vampires or other supernatural creatures would never hear them coming until it was too late. The Elite Daytime Guardians put the 'kill' in killer and fear into anyone that crossed them the wrong way.

Team Omega patrolled ever so quietly along the Bayou when a drunkard, Drunk Louie Carboni, fell off his electric blue bicycle into the bayou. Calvin told the other three with him, "Looks like ole Sampson and his gator children will be eating Italian tonight instead of Mexican." Drunk Louie tried desperately to climb ashore and cried out to the Elite Daytime Guardians to help him. They laughed as seven hungry alligators silently ambushed the drunkard. The gators, including Sampson, latched onto his legs, and slowly dragged him further and further away from shore. Drunk Louie Carboni screamed in terror as the gators tore him limb from limb. A torso-less Drunk Louie nearly passed out from the pain. Drunk Louie's adrenaline kept him wide awake, and Sampson ripped his head right off his shoulders with his massive gator jaws.

Shortly after the drunkard's misfortunate death there was loud screaming and yelling nearby the Esplanade Mansion. A large gather of humans approached the outside perimeter of the Esplanade Mansion. It was a group of degenerate hillbillies led by the triplets Crazy Britt, Trailer Swift, and Super Psycho Tiffy. The group consisted of the White family, a violent Asian woman plus those two dungeons and dragons idiots George and Tank Williams. Crazy Britt yelled outside the main entrance, "Come on outside Lord Alexander! We will no longer pay your vampire mafia 'protection money.' Fuck your Mystical Magical Kingdom. We came here to rob you like you robbed us week after week." Super Psycho Tiffy chimed in, "Lord Alexander, you kicked me out of the Esplanade Mansion. You had me thrown in prison on trumped up drug charges and stole my father's prized Shelby GT 500. I hate you and am going to cut your head off with a magic chainsaw!"

Kreaper arrived outside and told the strange midwestern cultists that the King of New Orleans was unavailable for comment and held the strange birds at gunpoint. Kreacher and the Elite Daytime Guardians tried to hold them at gunpoint, but a skirmish ensued. Kreaper ordered them shot in the legs and shot the chainsaws and pitchforks out of their mortal hands. The degenerate hillbillies cried out for justice but had gonorrhea panties stuffed in their mouths. The Elite Daytime Guardians bound their hands behind their backs and led them to the dungeons in the basement. The hillbillies tried to kick the King's Elite Daytime

Guardians but failed.

Kreaper pulled out a special iPad, pushed

three buttons, and the human trespassers

became chained with hardened steel

against their will. The steel chains hugged

them to wooden posts so they could not sit

or lay down. A fat redheaded woman

named Ashli complained of hunger pains

as they stood in their own waste for days.

The human slaves became mortified at

their predicament and cried out to their

false god Bally to save them. The steel

chains held them by their throats with their

feet barely touching the ground. Suppose

one of the hillbillies started to fall asleep.

Kreaper would force the degenerates to

listen to horrible Justin Beavers songs

until the humans tore their own hair out in

agony.

Lord Alexander's faithful butler, William

the dwarf, appeared out of thin air and

greeted the midwestern Bally cultists with a sinister laugh. William hung up ten portraits of Lord Alexander and the hot vampire ginger babes to torment the King's captives. The White father spoke out against this abuse, "You little fucker! Have you no decency? Please let us go in peace. We promise to never return to New Orleans, or this haunted Mansion again! I do not want my beloved White family to perish here. Please let us go. Please!"

William the dwarf chuckled at this White father and replied with an evil grin. "The Master of this Esplanade Mansion pays me very well in vampire gold. I cannot allow you to leave. I do not give two fucks whether your whole White family takes it up the ass every Thursday night! You Bally cultists will never become free. Expect some more demon dwarves to keep you company soon!" Later that evening William returned with twenty demonic dwarves.

William and his demonic brethren appeared and beat the piss out of the Bally cultists. The demonic dwarfs glared with their black eyes and forced enough piss infused grape drink down their throats to keep them barely alive. The evil dwarves grabbed baseball bats wrapped with razor wire and beat the Bally cultists unconscious. The Bally cultists longed for death, and the kiss of death did not find them. The Bally cultists cried out in sheer agony as the little demons tortured them physically and psychologically. The dwarves casted voodoo spells to keep them alive without food and boiled their skin with their wicked sorcery.

The fat redheaded woman Sunny cried out, "Please stop tormenting us humans. Are you little fuckers going to murder us tonight in this dreadful dungeon?" One of the demon dwarves kicked her repeatedly in the shins and laughed as Sunny's shin bones tore and grew exposed from the

violence by the demonic servants.

William, the leader of the demon dwarves

waved his wand, and everyone went dead

silent. William said, "Bitch, we demon

dwarves, have just gotten started

tormenting you depraved hillbillies.

Killing sounds too permanent lady. I am

the one who calls the shots!" William

stuck a gun in her fat mouth and educated

Sunny with a coldhearted passion. "I am

not a little fucker! I am the beginning to

your pain and the end to your freedom.

You can bend over and kiss your cheesecake goodbye!" William ordered the demon dwarves to force more grape piss down their throats and they slapped the Bally cultists with furious anger.

The demonic dwarves violently beat them increasingly and they began hallucinating colorful dragons picking apart their eyes and brains. Zarah Elizabeth Jackson appeared nude out of thin air with a bag full of shit flavored Midnight Potions.

Zarah said, "Drink my Midnight Potions little pretties." Zarah vanished after she handed the dwarves her special blended Midnight Potions. The demon dwarves forced the Bally cultists to drink the terrible version of Midnight Potions and the humans lost their hair and it fell to the stone floor. Later that night the Bally cultists began shrinking in size then growing. Fatter and skinnier. Skinnier and fatter. Their pain multiplied as their bodies shrank and grew in the cold dark dungeon.

William said to the Bally cultists in his deep demonic voice, "Ladies and gentlemen, I just don't like Mondays or fat yellow-bellied hippos on Prozac. Ta ta for now." Just like that William and the demonic dwarves vanished with the Bally cultists still chained to the wooden posts.

A week or so went by and Lord Alexander appeared before the Bally cultists in the dungeons with his favorite ginger vampire bitches, and the time was quarter past two

in the morning. The five ginger vampires

named, Mary, Margaret, Martha, Melanie,

and Madeline. They were the sexiest

goddamn redheaded green-eyed vampires

you ever laid your eyes upon. The five

vampires each had the palest and most

ashen colored skin you ever seen before.

Lord Alexander appeared before Crazy

Britt and Super Psycho Tiff. He swiftly

pimp slapped these cultist hoes like

nobody's business. The women called him a gangster and Lord Alexander did not like it. Lord Alexander educated these methed-up cultists and said, "I am not a gangster. I am a businessman, and my business is crime." Lord Alexander and the five ginger babes shouted, "The beatings will continue until morale improves! I locked you in my dungeon to teach you the ways of violent extortion methods of the vampire mafia." Super Psycho Tiff spat on the vampire king and said, "I should have killed you when you were still human."

Lord Alexander laughed as he thrusted his fist into her stomach and broke her spine in the process. Lord Alexander and his vampire babe assistants stuck a rifle in their mouths proclaiming, "Welcome to your first few weeks of Hell on Earth. Mary, Margaret, Martha, Melanie, and Madeline time to drink the fresh blood of these loser cultists."

The vampires ravaged the necks of the Bally cultists and sent their heads spinning metaphorically. The humans screamed with what little breath they had left in them. The cultists begged for release by the vampires or murdered to free them from the never-ending torment. Trailer Swift offered the King a good blowjob to escape the vampires. He chuckled and said, "Yeah those!" He punched Trailer Swift in the mouth and pulled out a vampire bat themed wand. Lord Alexander set her clothes ablaze with a special voodoo spell and the ginger vampires ripped her fiery clothes off and drained her blood some more. The humans were dazed and confused. Their situation made them realized that coming to New Orleans was a terrible idea concocted on bad meth smoked by a phony psychic crackhead named Shirley Brown.

Lord Alexander drained even more blood from the Bally cultists and told them, "The vampire mafia is not gangsters. We are simply businesspeople in the business of extortion, murder, prostitution, and racketeering. We vampires have every major politician and city council member paid from our deep pockets."

The Bally cultists trembled in fear as the vampires glared poisonous daggers in their direction. The King ordered his ginger vampire assistants to strip their clothes and valuables from their near lifeless bodies. The humans wept as they stared into the eyes of Satan and his demonic vampire babes.

Lord Alexander left the dungeon abruptly because his best friend the Vampire God Vincent telepathically summoned him again. Mary, Margaret, Martha, Melanie, and Madeline resumed torturing the poor humans. The King's assistants took the humans pain level to stage two. The ginger vampires gave the humans blood transfusions from diseased rats to keep them alive longer and prolong their torturous pain. The vampires were on strict orders from the King of New Orleans not to kill the humans. Lord Alexander wanted to kill the Bally cultists himself because murder and destruction were a huge part of his identity and psychological profile.

The ginger vampires forced the Bally cultists to drink a special witch's brew designed by the boozy and floozy witch Zarah. The special brew increased their life expectancy, and it also amplified their never-ending pain. It was a nightmare in which the Bally cultists could not escape. The Bally cultists prayed for forgiveness to the sadistic vampire mafia. Their false god Bally did not exist and was a legend brewed up on LSD mixed with false bible verses. Mary the leader of the five vampires spoke to the cultists, "I want you to keep praying to your false god! I want lightning and fire to crash down upon my fucking head!" The Bally cultists kept praying anyway.

George and Tank Williams tried to do mystical, magical, mountain magic to help them escape their clutches. The problem was George and Tank Williams had read their so-called magical mountain spells from a Mexican cookbook and thought it was a Latin Sorcery Bible. Mary and the other ginger vampires cut off George and Tank Williams' fingers and fed them to the demonic dwarves. George and Tank screamed like little bitches as the dwarves devoured their fingers one by one.

Melanie exclaimed, "Ginger sisters, the full moon appears much brighter after a proper feeding. We should fuck like there is not tomorrow and satisfy our sinful carnal desires!" Lord Alexander's five ginger vampire sex slaves danced on the rooftop of the Esplanade Mansion and ripped their clothes off. The green-eyed beauties danced furiously under the full moon and laughed maniacally as they kissed each other.

A hot warlock babe named Sam Jordan 0069 appeared out of thin air and beckoned the vampire babes to sleep with her on the rooftop. Sam Jordan 0069 was both a warlock and a top-level secret agent from the Order of the Leopard. Sam Jordan was five'8" and had platinum blonde hair, pale skin, toned body and a gorgeous white smile that could light up a galaxy.

The vampire babes and Sam Jordan scissor fucked and licked each other into an orgasmic oblivion. The Great Sorcerer Lou appeared, and he tried to join the all-female orgy, but his sexual advances were rebuffed and mocked by the women. He tried to cast a lust spell to entice them, but Secret Agent 0069 Sam Jordan stopped him dead in his tracks. Sam Jordan said,

"The Great Sorcerer Lou, this orgy is for sexy bitches only. Why don't you go to the Stoney Tavern on the first floor and drink on Lord Alexander's gold currency? Tell the barkeep Monika Stinson that Secret Agent 0069 sent you!" The Great Sorcerer Lou left, and he smashed on the King of New Orleans gold coin.

The gorgeous redheaded vampires took turns pleasuring Sam Jordan's lady love box with their succulent tongues. Mary said, "I have not had vagina taste this good since world war twice! This is mystical, magical coochie you have here Secret Agent 0069!" Sam Jordan replied, "Thanks babe, I trimmed it and washed it myself. Nobody wants to taste coochie that tastes like granny's shrimps!" The vampire babes playfully fought each other over who was going to drink and suck the juices of life from 0069 Sam Jordan's love box.

Downstairs The Great Lou drank the King's ultra-expensive 1942 Don Julio tequila. He told Monika the barkeep, "Man fuck dem hoes. I am only trying to get AAA ultra-premium pussy up in this motherfucker." Monika replied, "Those are the King's personal sluts and if he found out you tried to join their orgy, your ass would be grass and his fist in your face would be the lawnmower." The Great Lou drunk from intoxication chuckled and said, "The vampire King my ass. Fuck that motherfucker. I am The Great Lou and a great sorcerer. It should be me slapping

cheeks with dem fine ass hoes! How about

you pour me another shot of tequila and let

slide in balls deep in the backdoor!"

Monika replied, "Sorry Lou, my backdoor

is exit only and I have a boyfriend. How

about you try the nightclub Little Bitches

on Bourbon Street. You know dem short

college hoes will do anything for twenty

vampire coins." The Great Lou replied,

"Little Bitches you say? I have always

wanted to bang me a little midget fo sho! I

hope they got enough room for this black

anaconda. It is going in balls deep in that mother fucker!" The Great Lou left and banged all those little midget bitches.

THE DEATH CARD

Lord Alexander arrived at one of Vampire God Vincent's nightclubs called Fangs Be To God. The Vampire God gave Lord Alexander a rare scotch mixed with a splash of his potent God blood and Putin's children's tears. Vampire God blood was foreign to Lord Alexander as he only drank human and regular vampire blood. Vampire God Vincent took Lord Alexander to his VIP lounge and said, "Lord Alexander, there is much to discuss this evening, and I need you to sit down for this one." Lord Alexander sat down and was anxiously waiting further instruction from the Vampire God.

Chloe Murphy snuck past security and rudely interrupted the two vampires. Chloe yelled in the King's face and said, "Lord Alexander, your unholiness sir, I need a massive favor to ask of you please. I authored a book and tried to publish it a week ago…" Lord Alexander cut her off and exclaimed angrily, "Not now woman! I am super busy and engaged in the top-secret vampire mafia business that surpasses any human problem at this time. I have no time nor patience for silly human affairs!" Chloe pulled out a massive brown pouch full of vampire gold and shook the coins at the King. The vampire gold coins clinking together piqued Lord Alexander's interest quite a bit. He suddenly had time for this gorgeous gothic babe.

Chloe Murphy replied, "Lord Alexander, your Grace, I have a fuck ton of vampire gold here and will give you five bags of this shit to hear me out. I need you to 'take out' these five scumbag publisher agents who stole my literary work. They are making a fortune off my story. Their names are Adam Smith, Gregory Dukfuk, Monica Fieldlark, Kelsey Tomlinson, and James Bundy. I sent my work to Hairy Zebra Publishing, and these five low life pieces of shit stole my work. They used your lawn keeper Tommy 'Two Toes'

Maroni's name to authorize a backdoor

deal behind my back. These scoundrels

conspired and stole all my royalty

payments. I would be forever grateful to

you Lord Alexander if you can make these

scumbags pay! I authored a novel called; I

am Thrilled My Ex-Boyfriend Left Me

and Fucked My Grandpa In The Ass."

Lord Alexander interrupted her and

replied, "The Mad Dapper and vampire

King of New Orleans hears your prayers

for relief. I will grant their deaths on your

behalf, and you will have your rights

restored from these lecherous rats. I accept

your fealty and financial donation to the

King of New Orleans. Adam, Greg,

Monica, Kelsey, and James shall be in my

trunk by the end of the week. I, The Mad

Dapper, will personally murder the fuck

out of these vermin as this deserves a

special kind of violence for a special kind

of rat. I will drain their necks dry, stuff

maggots in their mouths and their lifeless

corpses will be swimming at the bottom of

the Mississippi River. The fish and gators

will feed on their lifeless bodies. Consider

this injustice corrected and your wealth

restored to you."

Lord Alexander summoned the five ginger

vampires in the middle of their orgy. He

gave them each two vampire coins and

sent them to kidnap the scumbag publisher

agents. Lord Alexander said, "All projects

are to be put aside and this will be your

new goal for the mafia King of New

Orleans. Mary, Margaret, Martha, Melanie, and Madeline drove off in the King's modified Porsche Macan S. They used their vampire iPads dubbed the Vampire Death pad and hacked the entire city's camera system to find the publisher agents. The facial recognition software dubbed Satan's All-Seeing-Eye and designed by the ORACLE spotted all five agents within a matter of seconds. The King kept his word and brutally murdered the humans with maggots stuffed in their dead mouths. Afterward the gingers disposed of their bodies in the Mississippi river, where Sampson's brother Hercules the tyrant alligator resided.

Lord Alexander returned to the Fangs Be To God nightclub and apologized to the Vampire God for disappearing in the middle of vampire mafia business. Vampire God Vincent told the King, you may be King of New Orleans and my vampire best friend but just remember who rules the world right now. I will take my 65% cut of that vampire gold you just scored. Do you play cards Lord Alexander? The house always wins more than the player." Vampire God Vincent snatched the gold right out of the King's hand and said, "This is not Fangs R Us motherfucker! This is Fangs R Me!" The two potent vampires had a good laugh.

Vampire God Vincent ensured the King was listening without interruptions this time by stationed to heavily bearded and tattooed werewolf bouncers outside his office. Vampire God Vincent told the King, "It has come to my attention that you massacred the leader of the transgender vampires, Princess Tiffanie. Thanks to you killing the gender bender vampire queen. It has sparked outrage in the rainbow section of the vampire community. A multitude of vampires, humans, dwarves, witches have gone missing or murdered. You inadvertently set off guerilla warfare where these gender bender degenerates are killing scores of innocent people. Pretty soon there will not be enough blood to go around New Orleans or even a pot to piss in. My latest intelligence report points to these gender-bending vampires overseeing all the disappearances and murders. That is why so many dead bodies float down the Bayou and the Mississippi river. I had the degenerates by their little balls. I had almost eradicated their abominable species from the earth. Your carelessness and impulsiveness know no bounds. I, the Vampire God, will strike more fear into this rainbow gender bender vampire

community once again. When you killed

of their leader, Princess Tiffanie, you

made the transgender vampires far

sneakier than we predicted and far more

difficult to track down and kill. I need you

to help me find their underground base of

operations in your sinful city. We need to

end this scummy transgender vampire

persuasion for the last time for the sake of

MY pure blood line. I went on a

worldwide nation-hopping campaign

conquering and killing their leaders. I

thought I finally made a dent in these gender-bending vampires. Frustration is an understatement. As you may not know, gender-bending vampires are far more robust and swifter than regular vampires. They could change their gender and appearance at will. It looks like you have forced the violent murderous anger in me yet again. We were going to kidnap and interrogate Princess Tiffanie to learn every base of operations. Thanks to your impulsive fuck up, I must attack this parasite race from a different direction."

Lord Alexander replied, "Yeah those! Suppose we kill every transgender vampire on the earth and wipe them off the map. What is next? Another robust enemy will rise like a hydra and take their place. You cut the head off one threat, and a new enemy appears from the abyss. We still do not know how potent the boozy and floozy witch, is either. I tried to fight her once in hand-to-hand combat, and she bested me with one arm tied behind her back. Zarah Jackson could have killed me but could not. Zarah is always in a drunkard state of mind and vomiting up cheap rum all over the place. I will help you gather the intelligence you need, and in turn, I implore you to gather more information on Zarah Elizabeth Jackson. I do not believe she is a simple baby making harlot witch that gets shitfaced every Saturday and Sunday night. I have a gut feeling she is not of this world and may have vast power beyond our capabilities."

Vampire God Vincent replied, "I will kill

this boozed-out bitch personally and kick
her worthless skull into a volcano to end
her miserable existence. I will inform you
of the boozy and floozy witch's weakness,
insane power and how she came into
being. We must eradicate Zarah and the
gender-bending vampires for the last time.
For the betterment of both our pure blood
line species and for humanity too. Less
chaos is good for vampire mafia
business."

Lord Alexander left the Fangs Be To God nightclub after the Vampire God dismissed him. Lord Alexander decided to visit his old gypsy friend Big Gay Salazar in the French Quarter. Big Gay Salazar was an old white guy with an Asian goatee, bald head, and a greasy hideous ponytail. Lord Alexander inquired about the weed strain and said, "Big Gay Salazar, that skunky funky pot you have their smells incredible! What in the fuck do you even call that shit?" Big Gay Salazar replied, "Oh this shit right here?

This shit right here? This is from my personal garden. It is one of the finest sativa herbs in the world, and I call it Past, Present, and Future. Suppose you inhale and smash this dank herb. It will get you so stoned that you can see your past, present, and future of course!" Lord Alexander replied and said, "Sorry, Big Gay Salazar, I only like smoking regular pot that doesn't screw up my immortal life and not have me talking to plants like Super Psycho Tiffy." Big Gay Salazar was so stoned he offered the King his fortune teller weed and ignored him anyway. Big Gay Salazar and Lord Alexander got higher than a Georgia Pine after toking off the bowl made of solid gold.

The King and gypsy were immediately transported to Chicago and the King was driving a rusty old car down Third Street and his human best friend Dustin was riding in the passenger seat. Big Gay Salazar was present too, but you could not see him. Big Gay Salazar spoke out of thin air, "Lord Alexander this happened in your past, and I need you to learn an important lesson here on this road." Lord Alexander and his black friend Dustin were higher than the life of Christ after smoking God's Gift before attending a work party during Christmas. They cruised down the street when they heard an old white witch cackling like the Devil in the distance. Lord Alexander and Dustin could not see the old white lady at first. As the horrifying demonic laughter grew louder and louder, a white SUV rolled up on them. It was a 2008 Cadillac Escalade with tricked out chrome rims, driving alongside them on the wrong side of the road. Lord Alexander looked at his black best friend and said, "Dust Master Flex this old white bitch is driving right next to us, and she has 1940 Tommy guns pointed at us." Dustin took another toke of the God's Gift weed and said, "Man, fuck that old white bitch and her white Cadillac Escalade. Oh, shit man! This bitch be trying to kill us bro. Watch out Alex, the evil lady is pumping this rust bucket full of lead!" Lord Alexander swerved all over the road and narrowly avoided a bullet to the face. The white SUV kept trying to ram the rusty car and the crazed old white woman cackled even louder as she pumped the rusty car full of lead.

Lord Alexander told Dustin, "We need to be getting the fucking fuck out of here, man. This old broad is going to kill us. We are about to cease to exist. I did not know smoking God's Gift weed would summon an old white woman demon from hell with an Escalade!" Lord Alexander stomped on the gas pedal, and they went over one hundred MPH. Dustin told Lord Alexander they could hide out in his apartment until the white SUV left. The white Escalade disappeared briefly and returned as soon as Lord Alexander parked. The crazed old white broad circled Lord Alexander and Dustin in the parking lot and begun firing her Tommy guns again. The old white woman laughed hysterically as she peppered bullets in their direction, narrowly missing them

with each trigger pull. The old white lady

said, "God and Satan sent me to kill you

both for smoking God's Gift!"

Dustin yanked Lord Alexander by the arm,

and they ran for their lives up the stairs to

Dustin's apartment. They were both so

high that neither Dustin nor Lord

Alexander could find the house key.

Dustin yelled at Lord Alexander standing

next to him and said, "Lord Alexander, I

cannot find my fucking house key. That SUV is going to murder us man. What do we do? What in the fucking hell do we do?" Lord Alexander replied, "Dust Master Flex, I am way too stoned to help you find your house key!"

Dustin laughed and said, "Lord Alexander you remember my DJ and street name but not my real name. You are not as high as you think you are my friend. We will find this lost house key or that ole white bitch will kill us. We must seek refuge in my

apartment man! I am way too high to die

right now. You can die if you want to fight

that demon from hell outside. Lord

Alexander saw a shimmering light in

Dustin's hand. "I found your keys Dust

Master Flex! They were in your fucking

hand this whole time." Dustin replied, how

in Merlin's beard did my keys end up in

my black hand?" Lord Alexander said,

"Who gives a shit how they got there! A

deranged psycho demon woman is still

shooting up the place!" The white SUV

faced the building, and that old crone peppered the whole apartment building with armor piercing ammunition. Thank God no innocent people were injured or killed by this crazy old broad. Lord Alexander grabbed Dustin's keys and was so high he kicked the door in after he could not figure out how to stick in and turn the key.

Lord Alexander told Dustin, "The crazy old white lady is finally gone! She and her white SUV are not in the parking lot

anymore!" Lord Alexander and Dustin felt

relieved for a moment. They sat in

Dustin's old worn-out leather chairs.

Dustin whipped out a fresh bowl of God's

Gift weed. Dustin looked at Lord

Alexander and said, "Hey man do you

want to get stoned off this bowl again? We

can take this weed to the next level of

highness my friend." Lord Alexander

replied, "Dustin, bro, I am already too

high, and we were nearly eradicated by the

white SUV. I do not think we can get any

higher my guy! Suppose we smoke our brains out that crazy bitch might show back up again and try to murder us."

Lord Alexander sat in Dustin's living room listening to Metallica and he heard Big Gay Salazar laughing hysterically in the background. Lord Alexander asked Dustin, "Hey do you hear someone in your apartment laughing right now?" Dustin replied, "I cannot hear anything but my hair growing right now! People be doing the freaky ass shit down the hall for a little

piece of change. Sometimes I can hear

moaning that sounds like two elephants

clapping cheeks and the walls shake with

an earthquake. I am waiting for my

computer to turn green so I can order us

Little Caesar's pizza." Lord Alexander

handed the funky skunky good shit to

Dustin so he could pack them another

bowl. The vampire and human smoked

their brains out and became one with the

universe. The two friends were so high

that they completely forgot about the white SUV that tried to murder them.

Lord Alexander asked Dustin, "Dusty did you order that pepperoni pizza yet bro?" Dustin replied, "My computer turned red and purple. It means the pizza joint closed on Mondays." Lord Alexander slapped him across the face and said, "For fucks sake man, it is Tuesday, not Monday. Get your shit together and order that cheap pizza. I got hoes I am trying to sleep with and chocolate to eat. I do not have time for this nonsense."

Lord Alexander left Dustin's apartment out of frustration with the pizza order. Lord Alexander sat in his rusty car, and it took him 15 minutes to figure out how to stick the key in the ignition and start the car. Big Gay Salazar appeared as an astral projection inside the car. He suggested to Lord Alexander, "Try pumping the gas pedal on that old piece of shit." After 20 tries the car miraculously started and died. On the 21st attempt it started right up and did not die. Lord Alexander asked the big gay fortune teller, "How do you keep popping up like this? Are you mystical and magical time travelling wizard?" Big Gay Salazar chuckled and said, "Lord Alexander the real question here is are you real, is this past event real, or are you just hallucinating and imagining me into existence?"

Lord Alexander was still high and heard the hairs on Big Gay Salazar's beard growing and multiplying like little rabbits. Lord Alexander begged Big Gay Salazar to switch seats and get them food. Lord Alexander looked in the rearview mirror and realized he was not a vampire in this past life but a human. Big Gay Salazar pulled out a Death Card from his fortune teller deck. He told Lord Alexander, "Ah, death! Death is my friend Lord Alexander. The white SUV of death should be your friend too. If what you are living for is not worth dying for, then find different

purpose in life." Lord Alexander rolled his

eyes as the fat man drove them to a cheap

diner in the hood at 2 am.

Big Gay Salazar was so gay he could not

drive straight and almost crashed the rusty

car into the white SUV which appeared

and disappeared. This time the white SUV

was driving itself with no crazy old

woman. Big Gay Salazar pulled out his

Past, Present, and Future weed and away

they toked. They shot back to the present and sat inside the Boozy and Floozy Witch goth bar. Everything happened in super slow motion. Time was not on why, why wasn't time on?

Lord Alexander and Big Gay Salazar ordered the infamous Midnight Potion drink, and they began tripping balls. The drink's hallucinogenic effects hit Lord Alexander at once. Zarah Jackson pulled out her purple crystal wand with a shiny red button and froze time. Zarah said to the King, "Lord Alexander, while you are drunk and high off my Midnight Potion, I will explain to you exactly what this cocktail holds. I brew up a special grape flavored witch's brew and mix it with LSD, magic mushrooms, 190 Ever Clear and a drop of my special wine. I want to thank you for introducing me to Lord Baar and his gay lovers years ago. I keep reproducing like a rabbit with these men of the bisexual persuasion. I created this Midnight Potion to control all humans especially men so I can breed with them.

You need to pay me child support since

these bisexual losers keep overdosing and

dying on me. Hope you enjoy that special

drink. I swirled in six drops from my lady

juices in there just for you, handsome."

Lord Alexander was dazed and confused

but still managed to grab the boozy and

floozy witch by her throat and he tried to

choke the life out of her. Zarah grabbed

both of Lord Alexander's hand with one

hand and flipped his massive vampire frame onto the stone floor in the bar's courtyard. Lord Alexander looked up and his life flashed before his eyes. Zarah appeared to have red and purple lizards growing from her hair and eyeballs. Lord Alexander said to himself that this could not be real. Zarah punched and stomped the vampire King until he was almost unconscious. She dragged him to the upstairs bar where Marilyn Manson is known to frequent around Halloween. Zarah ripped off the King's blue Canali suit and carefully hung it up. Zarah sucked

the King's massive dick, and she

conquered him. The King did not seem to

mind the lustful clutches of the boozy and

floozy witch. They fucked and passed out

in the cage until sunrise.

Two hours had passed, and the King

finally snapped back to reality and found

his suit hung up, his Versace boxers on

backwards and his favorite 14k gold onyx

pinky ring missing in action. Lord

Alexander had no recollection of what just took place and was sober after the Midnight Potion wore off. He regained all his strength and stamina and searched for the witch to find his ring.

Meanwhile Big Gay Salazar continued to smoke his Past, Present, and Future weed in the courtyard. The special weed gave him his fortune teller abilities. Big Gay Salazar read the palms of five young men inside the bar and found one that fancied him. He took him by the wrist and read his

fortune to him. Big Gay Salazar said,

"Look here Kirk, this crooked line

extending to your pinky means you are of

the bisexual persuasion, and you have

deeply hidden gay tendencies. I can teach

you the ways of the gay and show you

how deep your little booty hole goes

tonight."

Kirk was angry at this big gay gypsy

fortune teller as he tried to lure him to bed

from the bar. Kirk shouted, "Listen Linda, listen Linda, I do not swing that way, and I do not appreciate you pushing your creepy homosexual agenda onto me." Big Gay Salazar smirked and pulled out a fortune teller tarot deck full of Death cards. He told the young man, Kirk, to pick a card and he will predict his future coming in the next week. Kirk pulled the Death card of course and Kirk's college friends teased him about dying.

Big Gay Salazar always get his man, so he threw his infamous red and white gypsy powder in Kirk's face. Time briefly froze and a lecherous Salazar whispered into Kirk's ear. Kirk was stone faced but his eyes spelled out mortified. Big Gay Salazar told Kirk he would be his companion for all eternity. Kirk hypnotized by Big Gay Salazar's powder and obeyed his lecherous captor. The five college boys left the Boozy and Floozy witch bar with Big Gay Salazar. He introduced Kirk to the gay persuasion

while Kirk's friends beat off in the closet.

Lord Alexander kicked in Big Gay

Salazar's apartment door and approached

the gay gypsy. Big Gay Salazar said to the

King, "Tough night Lord Alexander? Your

face is black and blue and smells like

lovely lady honey juice. Did you forget

where you were again?" Lord Alexander

replied, "I have no recollection of going to

the bar or losing my favorite gold onyx

pinky ring. I need to go back to the Boozy and Floozy witch before sunrise to collect my protection money from Zarah Jackson."

Big Gay Salazar choked on his bowl of weed and coughed out bluish green smoke on the exhale. The gypsy said, "Big Gay Salazar sees all and is psychic. I saw you drink the Midnight Potion have sex with Psycho Zarah and she ripped off your pinky ring when you passed out. Zarah does that to everyone to feed her cocaine addiction. You really are one careless motherfucker to be sleeping with that sleazy hoe. Lord Alexander you should be more careful as to whom you stick your pecker inside. Do you know what I mean jellybean?"

Lord Alexander said, "I know this gypsy, I will head there in a moment and extort that bitch and take more vampire gold for protection this time. I do not care how good in bed she is or what kind of combat

skill she has in her bones. Zarah will pay

the vampire mafia extortion or die!" Big

Gay Salazar chuckled and said, "Lord

Alexander she beat the britches off you

my lord and put your Versace underwear

on backwards. I do not think you stand a

chance going up against Zarah and getting

your protection money or pinky ring

back." Lord Alexander smirked and said,

"She may be boozy and floozy with good

coochie and warrior hands. I will bring my

gingers and stuff her in the trunk of my

Porsche Macan. I will get my goddamn gold ring back tonight or die trying!"

Big Gay Salazar told the King, "Lord Alexander, I do not think you will be collecting any vampire gold tonight. Zarah beat you stupid and blew your balls off with her cum guzzler. You are in way over your head on this one trust me bitch. I see how you look at her though with those cold dark eyes of yours. You are madly in love with that witch." Lord Alexander replied, "Where the hell were you while Zarah was draining my balls and making a fool out of me? You could not stop her with your potent crystal ball or dank ass weed?" Big Gay Salazar said, "I chase dick. Pussy is your problem vampire King. Suppose you paid me in weed I could take care of that problem for you or just watch you suffer from the love spell she put on you. You are under her control, and she does not love you back. Zarah does that to all vampires she crushes on but does not have true feelings for them."

Lord Alexander spread his silver wings and flew back to the Boozy and Floozy Witch bar. Lord Alexander asked the bar patrons if they had seen Zarah Jackson. The town drunkard and full-time bumbling idiot spoke up. Andrew Carnahan said he saw Zarah Jackson snorting cocaine with agent 0069 Sam Jordan near the main entrance to the upstairs bar. Lord Alexander said, "Fear not drunkard, I will not kill you. I am trying to recover my favorite pinky ring. Was Zarah wearing the gold ring adorned with a black onyx stone when she was snorting coke?" The drunkard tried to answer the King but passed out from too many drinks. Andrew slept with his hand down his pants and pissed all over himself. The King punched him ferociously in the stomach and Andrew wet himself again and did not wake back up.

Lord Alexander grew infuriated by Zarah's theft, and she was flaunting the King's pinky ring around the bar. Zarah Jackson was doing line after line with Sam Jordan and had not a care in the world. Lord Alexander's temper had flared, and he sprinted toward her at an ungodly speed. He said, "I demand my ring back woman. Hand it over and I will not kill you before sunrise."

Zarah Jackson was selling hearty hand jobs with her left hand and blowing coke with her right hand. Zarah Jackson took a swig of Johnnie Walker double black out of her private stash and unleashed a relentless assault on the King of New Orleans. The King easily dodged Zarah's blows since he now had God blood flowing through his immortal veins. The Vampire God blood changed his aura and wings to golden in appearance. Lord Alexander now had close to the same speed and strength as Vincent.

Lord Alexander caught Zarah Jackson off guard and penetrated her defense. He hit her with a Mortal Kombat upper cut to the jaw and hurled her into the ceiling, and she hit the hickory floor, hard. Lord Alexander snatched his striking gold pinky ring off her finger with ease. Zarah Jackso screamed, "Who in the hell do you think you are hitting a lady???" Lord Alexander smirked and said, "Zarah, you are no lady for wreaking havoc in MY city! Zarah Jackson, you part-time lover, are a public nuisance to society. You are a rabid dog that must be put to death for good! I am sick and tired of you roaming the city and spreading your legs to the very men you rob. I will be summoning my gingers to deal with your trifling ass." Lord Alexander summoned the gingers with his mind to deal with Zarah Jackson. Lord Alexander ordered the gingers to hogtie the boozy and floozy witch and forced her inside the Porsche Macan S's back seat. The ginger assistants took Zarah Jackson to the Esplanade Mansion, so Zarah, could be tortured alongside the Bally cultists.

Lord Alexander's final instructions were to kill off Zarah and the Bally cultists and feed their dead bodies to Sampson in the bayou.

The five gingers dragged a screaming Zarah to the dungeon and strapped her to a wooden pole. The gingers placed a unique bandage blessed by the Voodoo Queen, Dawn Lightfoot, on Zarah's mouth so she could not curse them with words or her devilish gaze. The gingers left the

Mansion in the King's Porsche, and ten homeless junkies blocked their path. Zelda the dwarf was driving and slammed on the brakes to avoid damaging Mr. Porsche.

Mary pressed the window button and rolled it down. She shouted, "Attention, all junkies! Attention, all junkies! We have top-secret business that supersedes any plans you heroin addicts have for this road." Mystical Homeless Jesus, the junkie's leader, shouted, "Fuck you lady!

You are in New Orleans and only the strongest survive in this city!" Mary firmly told the dwarf drive to park Mr. Porsche, and she got out of the Macan. The junkies were fucked up on heroin did not realize Mary was seven foot tall or a powerful vampire. The gutter punk junkies started screaming incoherent nonsense and tried to hit the vampire babe with their stolen bicycle locks. Mary and her sisters punched the drug addicts so hard in the face that their heads flew clean off their shoulders.

The gingers chuckled as the picked up the heads of the gutter punks and kissed them all on the mouth. Mary said, "See girls that was easy breezy. These junkies' heads would add a nice touch to the dungeon. Let us carry them to the dungeon and give the Bally cultists something to cry about." The vampire babes drained the blood still squirting out of their neck stumps before tossing the torsos in the bayou. They kicked their bodies in the water and

Sampson and his children ate the corpses swiftly and eagerly.

The five gingers made it back to the Esplanade Mansion after taking kickbacks from a city councilwoman named Jalisa North. Their vampire mafia business was not delayed for too long by the street walking junkies. The gingers escorted Zarah Jackson to the dungeon and tossed her on a separate pole next to the Bally cultists. Zarah was strapped to a pole, which was cursed by the King's best

friend, the Voodoo Queen of New

Orleans. Zarah was unable to bless or

curse her way out of this trouble. Zarah

screamed and kicked the pole to no avail.

A SATAN POWERED 1969 CORVETTE

427

Lord Alexander had a flashback of his human sister Jennifer McBride. Jennifer played a board game from the 1980's called Mall Madness, leading her to make terrible decisions as an adult. Lord Alexander chuckled loudly as he remembered Jennifer playing this game and ruining her life. Thanks to this game called Mall Madness, Jennifer grew up and became a lecherous whore that shopped at every mall in America. This cursed boardgame was the reason Jennifer

had five baby daddies and about ten

boyfriends she slept with every other day.

She could not keep a man around to save

her depraved broke soul.

The Mall Madness boardgame created by

Satan lead little children into committing

the seven deadly sins. Satan offered the

boardgame to the CEO of Milton Bradley

in exchange for his pathetic human soul.

Satan ordered the CEO to sign the wealth

contract in his own blood to solidify their business partnership. Satan and his demons cursed each game that Milton Bradley sold to the public. Every major retailer in North America sold this despicable boardgame. Mall Madness tricked every teenage girl into worshipping Satan, having premarital sex and drugs beyond human comprehension. Suppose you need a real reason to blame Milton Bradley and Satan for your daughter or sister growing up to being a gluttonous baby maker, a credit card fiend,

and utterly useless to society, the answer is
Mall Madness.

Jennifer eventually had a total of ten
children by ten different men and cannot
manage her finances as an adult. Jennifer
was cursed by playing this stupid
boardgame from hell. Mall Madness
taught Jennifer to be more greedy, lustful,
prideful, wrathful, envious of thy
neighbor, and became a deadweight sloth.
Jennifer hopped from man to man draining

their bank accounts dry. She became a money-grubbing multi-platinum depressed super slut thanks to this game designed by Satan. Jennifer whored her way across America, especially the Midwest, Southwest, and Northeast.

Jennifer made triple the money from desperate men because she lost all her teeth from her crack addiction. Jennifer stole men's' credit cards, gold coins and anything she could get her grubby paws on to pawn. Jennifer bought herself expensive

clothes, caviar, and a fancy Lambo which

had been repossessed by the IRS to pay

back taxes.

Capital Two which used to be Capital One

repossessed the Lambo since she only

spent her ill-gotten fortune without saving

or investing for a rainy day. Capital One

became Capital Two after they refused to

pay Chuck Norris for protection money

against the federal government. Chuck

Norris stormed into Capital One's CEO's office and round house kicked that cock sucker into next month. That is the story behind how Capital Two came to be.

Secret Agent 0069 Sam Jordan discovered that Capital Two was paying kickbacks to Chuck Norris and informed Lord Alexander. With this information Lord Alexander extorted the CEO of Capital Two and offered him protection from Chuck Norris. Lord Alexander said, "Tom, you will pay me 65% of your back-end business dealings and funnel the money through my Italian restaurant business. In exchange I will keep the monkey off your back and protect you from that bad ass Chuck Norris." Tom Hilton eagerly agreed since Chuck Norris was not to be trifled with in society. Chuck Norris was banging Tom's wife every Tuesday and Wednesday on the table where he eats his Salisbury steak dinner with corn.

Mall madness was the greatest selling board game from 1989-2005 until Monopoly took the crown. Lord Alexander enriched his vampire mafia empire thanks to all the bribes and kickbacks Tom Hilton paid to keep the 'Don't Fuck With Chuck' fellow at bay. The public was unaware the Devil designed Mall Madness or Monopoly until today. The gingers would show up every Saturday to collect the extortion payments to keep the secret of Tom's soul selling shame a secret to the world. Tom sold his soul twice if you factor in Lord Alexander protecting him from Chuck Norris.

Fast forward to present day after the memory recall. Lord Alexander paced up and down Bayou St. John seeking drunkards and drug addicts to brutally murder and feed upon nightly. Depending on the King's mood he either killed them with his sword or ripped their heads off with his bare hands. Lord Alexander always tossed the dead bodies in the bayou to feed his pet alligator Sampson and his

magnificent children. Any drunk Louie's

or methed-up Mary's went straight to

Sampson after the King got his cut of the

blood and carnage.

Sampson was an incredibly happy

alligator that liked to perform circus like

tricks for anyone passing by the bayou.

Lord Alexander and the public enjoyed

tossing a basketball to Sampson and he

would swat the ball back with his

significant tail. Tourists from around the world would marvel at the size of Sampson and his gator children. They would take pictures with him and sang him songs to soothe him to sleep.

One scorching evening, Lord Alexander, tossed Sampson a fresh body and heard the loudest Corvette 427 on the planet. The marvelous 1969 Corvette soared by Lord Alexander on Moss Street. The paint and headlights blacked out by Vincent.

Purple and black demon skulls and hell fire flames exited the car's solid gold exhaust system. Lord Alexander felt a sense of dread as the tinted car kept circling around the block. He felt uneasy as he thought it was a rival faction coming to challenge him for the throne. Lord Alexander's thoughts raced as murder, death and chaos ran through his immortal mind.

The unknown driver of the 1969 Corvette parked in the fire lane of the Esplanade Mansion. Lord Alexander with the speed of a fallen angel sprinted directly toward the car ready for war. He tried to get a glimpse inside the glorious Vette. The super car's windows were blacked out and blocked any visibility from the outside. Lord Alexander could not penetrate the tint with his Vampire God eyes. Lord Alexander exclaimed, "Who is trespassing at my Mystical, Magical Mansion?" Vincent appeared from the 1969 Corvette all suited up in a Brioni outfit with a hot goth babe in her mid-twenties. "Relax, Lord Alexander, its just God, doing God's work. I picked up this cute hooker for you and me to share this scorching evening. She comes with handles on her head. Check out the pigtails on this bodacious broad! One of the Elite Daytime Guardians told me you like sexy bitches that come equipped with blowjob handlebars and here we are." Lord Alexander was relieved to see the Vampire God and not the werewolf cartel. This meant no more killing this evening and Lord Alexander would be able to enjoy sex by the campfire all night.

Vampire God Vincent stood at the same height as the King. Ten feet and zero inches. He had blonde hair pulled back in a ponytail and a snarl that would make the Prince of Demon's jealous. Vincent replied, "Yeah, those! I brought you this gorgeous babe to blow our balls off tonight and we are going to drink her blood like a couple of people who are in charge around here! I wanted to show you my new toy that I tactfully acquired after I killed Lord Mammon, who was one of the princes of Hell. That little cocksucker refused to pay up after I beat him in poker. The second time this week that this bullshit happened. So, I killed the bastard and took his Vette as payment for trying to skirt out of paying up. I drank that fucker's blood, and it tasted a bit like pineapple juice mixed with Columbian cocaine. I threw his unholy corpse into a woodchipper to strike fear into those

demon princes to show them I rule the

world not Satan and his minions. The

custom exhaust system made of pure gold

is louder than Christ screaming on the

cross. It is bad to the bone, and I will tell

you about this super car's features. Satan

Fuel powers the motor, and I fused Prince

Mammon's unholy soul to the car. Mrs.

Vette has the fastest 0-60 time anywhere

in the world. Lord Alexander, you may

never get the chance to drive this hot rod

from hell. Suppose you drive it without

my permission another soul will be installed inside the motor."

After Vincent's story, Lord Alexander challenged him to a duel since he believed his power was now equal to the Vampire God. It was hugely different from what Vincent possessed and he got his ass whooped harder than Connor McGregor talking shit to Lesnar. Lord Alexander was mesmerized by Vincent's strength and hand-to-hand combat skills and dreamed of one day being on par with the original Vampire God.

Lord Alexander exclaimed, "Who needs Mrs. Vette? I can fit more sexy bitches in Mr. Porsche! Vinny, I want you to take a long hard look inside Mr. Porsche. I can fit four or five bitches in this motherfucker and three in the trunk no problem." Sam Jordan was walking by them and said, "Lord Alexander and Vincent, are we going to screw that babe with the blowjob-handles or what? Quit measuring your dicks over whose car is better and let us get on with the baby making! I need twins up in this tight bitch pussy!" Lord Alexander was too busy arguing with Vincent to pay attention to the human women. Whose car was better argument led to another fist fight between the two immortal blood sucking gods. Vincent pummeled the King again even though he managed to strike him four times in the face. Lord Alexander's new potent god power was no match for Vincent, the first

of their kind.

Lord Alexander said, "Lord Vincent, let

me school you on what this badass Macan

S can do. It has Lord Baar's soul infused

permanently under the hood. It has a

ludicrous Zeus mode that can also reach 0-

60 in a fraction of a second. I fuel this

bitch up with a secret blend of Boozy and

Floozy fuel, and Zarah's Midnight Potions

which I stole from her bar. I also put in the

blood of Zarah's murdered bisexual lovers as an oil additive to keep the engine running cooler than usual. How about we race our cars down Broad Street and the winner gets the other car? The pig tailed goth babe Nicole Maroni sat in the Macan S and Sam Jordan sat in Mrs. Vette.

The race took place at three in the morning, started at Canal Street and finished at the Esplanade Mansion. The potent original god rolled down his window and said, "Mrs. Vette will beat the britches off that piece of shit German car. After I win, I will be taking that Macan S to the incinerator, and you will have to call me Don Steel or Godfather. Since I am the one who rules this beautiful world, not you." Lord Alexander flipped Vincent off and said, "Vinny, you may be God, but you are crazy if you think that Vette will beat Mr. Porsche in a street race! You are crazier than four bed bugs smoking crack on a Friday!"

Lord Vincent replied, "I am crazy. Everybody including my ex-wife, Shirley Leonidas, calls me crazy. Before Christ was crucified by that Pilate fellow and rose from the dead. Being crazy used to mean something. Nowadays everybody including my swamp demon sister, Morganna are crazy! You merely tasted the god blood flowing through your veins. It is a modicum of the power I own within this ancient and prehistoric carcass. You will lose this street race. I might even take

both these hot goth babes to your

penthouse and fuck them good in YOUR

bed as an insult to injury."

Lord Alexander replied, "Not the hot goth

babes in my bed. Not unless it is me. I do

not get fucked racing on the streets. I do

the fucking!" Lord Vincent said with a

smirk, "We need to hurry this race along

and quit bragging. I am on a mission to

kill Vladimir Putin since he is the new

world leader of the gender-bender

vampires, called the Deadly Switchers." Lord Alexander was intrigued by the secret name of the transgender vampire community. He asked, "What the hell is a Deadly Switcher?" Lord Vincent quickly answered: "I guess your drunk ass, did not get the memo I sent a week ago, through the slow dwarf mail. The Deadly Switchers are what these transgender transformer vampires are calling themselves now. The gender benders changed their name and went deep underground which made it harder to track them with the technology we bought from the ORACLE. After you killed their leader Princess Tiffanie, they waged war against the world."

Lord Alexander was in shock that the vampire mafia was now at war with these degenerate Deadly Switchers. The transgender vampires are half android and half vampire but far stronger than both species. The android part of their bodies is what makes them so hard to kill. Lord

Baar purposely misled Lord Alexander into believing they were typical vampires that could switch genders at will.

The ORACLE uncovered and stopped a plot in which Lord Alexander and Lord Vincent were to be assassinated by the Deadly Switchers. The Deadly Switchers goal was to eradicate pure blood vampires and humans and transform everyone into their species including animals. Lord Alexander drove them even further underground and the Deadly Switchers are

murdering innocent civilians in New

Orleans and throughout the world. Lord

Vincent said, "I will infiltrate Russia and

assassinate Putin to cut the head off the

snake. Princess Tiffanie and Comrade

Putin were the mad scientists that created

the species of abomination. Lord Baar

stole money from me to fund these

experiments and gave birth to a potent far

leftist movement as a contingency plan in

case Lord Baar was murdered by you,

Lord Alexander."

Lord Alexander felt a sense of dread and was deeply troubled with Lord Vincent's speech. Lord Alexander began to question his own reality as King. He feared his own assassination by the Deadly Switchers or an ally of theirs.

After a brief road race to the Esplanade Mansion, Lord Alexander lost to Lord Vincent. Lord Alexander screamed in his potent deep voice, "Fuck you and Mrs. Vette. You cheat son of a bitch got a quarter second head start." Lord Vincent

waved his hand and silenced the King. He

said, "Enough squabbling about our super

cars. I only got TWO INCHES OF SLEEP

since I began my Deadly Switcher

eradication. I must complete my mission

to wipe them from the face of the earth.

While you are always too busy whoring

around town, I am out killing transgender

vampires with my sword."

Lord Alexander was shocked, and Lord Vincent forgot to collect the King's Porsche as a prize. Lord Vincent in a hurry left in Mrs. Vette and peeled out like a bat out of hell. Lord Alexander had intruders to torture and kill. He forgot about the Deadly Switchers and wished to resume his torture of the Bally Cultists and Zarah Elizabeth Jackson. Lord Alexander also had pussy on his mind and sent the gingers to continue the torturing and killing of the humans.

Lord Alexander briefly bade good night to the vampires, humans, and dwarves that inhabited the Esplanade Mansion. He took the pigtailed goth babe Nicole and Secret Agent 0069 Sam Jordan to his bed chambers. The King wished to wax their love boxes all week long! He needed stress relief after hearing about the secret Deadly Switcher war.

Lord Alexander asked the goth babe, "Nicole, sweety, does the carpet match the black drapes?" Nicole laughed extremely hard and said, "What carpet? I shave my little birdie bald as a cucumber!" Sam Jordan said the same about her beautiful coochie box. The King became aroused as these humans stripped to their naked flesh. He gazed upon their succulent and marvelous breasts with their perfect pink nipples. Lord Alexander's prick grew thicker and longer as he watched the two

goth babes suck each other's tongues in
front of him.

Lord Alexander was so fascinated with the
two human women that he debated on
transforming them into vampires that
evening. Lord Alexander asked them both
if they were interested in becoming
immortal to stay young and beautiful
forever. Lord Alexander said, "Sam
Jordan and Nicole Maroni are you
interested in becoming my vampire brides

tonight? Do you eat canned spaghetti more than twice a week? The smell of canned spaghetti is extremely repulsive thanks to my old human lover Kelsey Thompson eating that bootyhole shit every day of the week." The women declined the King's invitation to become immortal and a knock heard by the trio at the King's penthouse door startled them.

Dawn Lightfoot the reigning Voodoo Queen of New Orleans was standing in the penthouse doorway nude. Dawn asked if she could join the threesome full of sex and debauchery. The vampire King eagerly allowed her into the penthouse and his butler, William, made them all rum punches. The immortal and humans drank the rum punch and 1942 Don Julio Primavera tequila and screwed hardcore.

The King licked and sucked their succulent breasts, and the gorgeous women took turns taking the King's cock

in their small human mouths. Sam Jordan
and Dawn Lightfoot scissored on the bed
and Dawn Lightfoot sat on the King's face
and melted into pure ecstasy from the oral
pleasures of life.

The King and human women melted
passionately into each other's arms and
afterward he led the women to the throne
room on the seventh floor overlooking St.
Louis Cemetery #3 and downtown New
Orleans. Nicole Maroni and the other two

women sat nude on the floor. Lord Alexander beckoned Nicole Maroni to rise from the floor. The five ginger vampires appeared carrying a gold chalice filled with tequila and the King's blood.

The ten-foot-tall god caused Nicole Maroni to kneel on both naked knees before Lord Alexander's throne. The other two humans continued to kiss and declined immortality. Nicole Maroni was incredibly nervous since the icy cold throne room hardened her nipples like steel. Lord Alexander stretched out his long pale left hand with his palm facing up. Lord Alexander looked at the gingers and said, "Mary, you will bring forth the King's precious gold chalice filled with my potent blood and tequila. Margaret, you will present the King's dagger!" The two gingers followed the King's orders. William and three demonic dwarves appeared out of thin air and brought Nicole Maroni a black silk dress adorned with red vampire bats hand stitched into the fabric.

The ginger vampires and demonic dwarves went into a trance like state and began dancing furiously around Lord Alexander and his vampire bride to be. Lord Alexander took the gold chalice raised it to the heavens and said, "Nicole Maroni, drink this god blood! For it is the blood of your future and is the key to your new reality. After you drink from this chalice, you will die for an hour and be reborn into my student of the dark. Suppose you refuse the immortality I offer you tonight. I will have the gingers cut your head off with a chainsaw and mail your head to your family back in New York City."

After the King gave his immortal speech, Nicole Maroni was shaken with fear and anxiety. Either way she would die tonight. Nicole, kneeling on both naked knees stretched out her pale human hands and took the gold chalice from the King's hands. Nicole pressed the cup to her lips and drank the King's blood. Shortly after this took place Nicole's head started spinning and she knew that she was dying.

Nicole tried to stand up but fell to floor and her eyes rolled back in her head as if she were having a seizure. Nicole's mind started racing at first for ten minutes. Next her mind slowed down, and her breathing ceased. During her last few moments of

life as a human she felt terror and agony as

the blood seemed like poison burning

throughout her body.

Lord Alexander smirked and laughed as

Nicole Maroni died from his immortal

blood. Lord Vincent appeared from the

chimney and sat next to Lord Alexander

for a moment. Lord Vincent spoke to

Nicole and said, "After you are dead for

one hour, you will be reborn into your

everlasting future." Lord Alexander

appeared confused that Lord Vincent was

there for the immortal transformation

ceremony. He said, "Lord Vincent, I

thought you were out murdering Deadly

Switchers throughout the world. What are

you doing here this evening?" Lord

Vincent replied, "I am here to see the

unholy matrimony of the King of New

Orleans and his goth babe bride. I happen

to be a very resourceful god when it comes

to keeping up with your activities. My

methods are supernatural and far beyond

comprehension. Murdering all these transgender degenerates has begun to bore me a bit. I wanted to see something more positive for a change other than Deadly Switchers strewn about the cities. I have important intelligence to share with you after Nicole arises from the dead."

Lord Vincent gave Lord Alexander a large goblet filled with only his blood to give Lord Alexander more of his god power. Lord Alexander died in a comparable manner to Nicole Maroni and arose from death quicker than she did. Lord Alexander lost any trace of his silver aura and wings, and both were now pure gold in color.

Nicole Maroni was reborn into a mystical, magical vampire and she sported half gold and silver wings and aura. She grew from five foot eight to eight feet in height. Her appearance remained like her human form except her skin became paper white and the veins more visible in Nicole's face.

The King's vampire priest Ka-Ching married the two immortals as soon as Nicole was able to stand up without falling on the ground. Ka-Ching was both vampire priest and an accountant to the King of New Orleans. Ka-Ching's job was to pay everyone their wages in gold from all vampire mafia business. Ka-Ching's side hustle was fucking werewolf and witch bankers out of gold and getting away with it.

Lord Vincent ordered Ka-Ching to go extort bankers on Wall Street in New York City. Ka-Ching left, and Lord Vincent celebrated with the newlywed vampire couple. Lord Vincent was so thrilled with Lord Alexander's decision to turn Nicole into the undead. He inquired about Dawn Lightfoot and Secret Agent 0069. Lord Alexander said they were not interested in becoming immortal and Nicole Maroni

had no choice.

Lord Vincent threw Lord Alexander the

keys to Mrs. Vette and said, "Take this

demonic car as a wedding gift and do all

the sex for both of us. I have not been

married since world war twice when I was

out killing Nazis and skull fucking their

corpses. Lord Alexander one day and that

day may never come. I will call upon you

to do a service for me. Until that day

comes, accept your new god power, and

blacked out 1969 Corvette as a gift stolen

from devils." The King told Lord Vincent,

"This is your most prized possession. This

1969 Corvette is your pride and joy. You

went to hell and killed Mammon to obtain

this super car. What deed have I conducted

to deserve such generosity from the

original vampire god?"

Lord Vincent replied, "Lord Alexander,

you make me the most gold in comparison

to the other vampire Kings. I am the

Godfather of all our kind, and you happen

to be my most favorite offspring. I am a

generous god who felt the King of New

Orleans deserved something faster than

that piece of shit Porsche you drive." The

two friends laughed and laughed about fast

cars and killing Deadly Switchers.

Lord Vincent stood up and addressed

everyone in the room with authority. Lord

Vincent ordered anyone not a vampire to

leave the room. He then said, "I am on my way to murder Putin and his Deadly Switcher persuasion in Russia. That should give Ukraine relief from that evil tyrant. I will destroy that scumbag since he is terrorizing innocent civilians and raping them in Ukraine. Putin is trying to cover up his misdeeds, but I have exposed his plot to the ORACLE. Zarah Jackson escaped your prison you made for her. One other thing Lord Alexander, Terry the werewolf, said he attended one of your full moon pool parties last month. A Don does not wear shorts."

Lord Alexander grew infuriated that Zarah Jackson escaped from her voodoo powered pole. Before Lord Alexander could order the gingers, and Elite Daytime Guardians, to search for her trifling ass he received an unexpected phone call from his human sister Jennifer.

Jennifer McBride was hammered as usual

and probably methed-up again. She

screamed, "The worst Jessica used to call

me at four in the morning claiming

dragons were flying out of her closet to eat

her brain. Rebecca's are sometimes gay

when drunk but strictly dickly when

sober!" Lord Alexander looked at his

iPhone in disgust and said, "Not now

woman! I am hunting the boozy and

floozy witch plus trying to kill these

cultists. You always call me when you are

shitfaced and at the worst inopportune

time. Just convert every Jessica and

Rebecca into your lesbian persuasion and

leave me in peace!"

THE DEADLY SWITCHERS AND A PLANNED RESURRECTION?

Comrade Putin and the Russians invaded Ukraine based on false pretenses and to overthrow the Ukrainian leadership. Comrade Putin lied to his own people and said he needed to de-nazify Ukraine and to join their Country with the Communists. Comrade Putin planned to take over every country on earth or wipe them off the map with nukes. Comrade Putin had become the sole leader of the Deadly Switchers

after Lord Alexander brutally executed

Princess Tiffanie with his sword.

Comrade Putin kept up the

experimentation of transforming both

humans and vampires into the Deadly

Switcher persuasion. The elite intelligence

group known as the ORACLE infiltrated

Russia and found a talker. One of the

leaders of the ORACLE offered the

unknown gender bender vampire a spiked

bloody beverage laced with truth serum,

and it disclosed information about the

Deadly Switchers plans for world

domination.

The ORACLE had the gender bender

immortal convinced she was one of their

kind. The leader of the ORACLE

temporarily changed her appearance to

exude a rainbow aura with a top-secret

iPhone application designed at their

headquarters. The phone app also changed

her voice to sound like a half male and

half female untuned Satanic Music Box.

The app also changed the leader's clothes

into the Deadly Switcher signature outfit.

This consisted of a rainbow and sparkly

dress with a prosthetic horse leg hanging

out a side hole in the dress. The ORACLE

leader asked the Deadly Switcher, "What

are the goals for us Deadly Switchers and

how many of 'us' are there in the world?"

The hypnotized, and drunkard gender-bender replied, "Comrade Putin enslaved an entire family of witches, scientists, and dragons. They were forced to use ancient Haitian voodoo and advanced A.I. technology to give birth to our gender-bending hybrid species. Princess Tiffanie and Comrade Putin created our half vampire and android species in defiance of Lord Vincent's pure blood decree. The Vampire God wishes to rule the entire universe with an iron fist, and he will kill us rainbow people to achieve his goals. The original two of our kind secretly created us a hundred years ago in a lab to

rival the strength and power of the original

Vampire God. Comrade Putin ordered six

prostitutes to get Lord Vincent drunk to

collect DNA samples from his ancient

blood. Half of our body and brain is

android and the other half vampire. Our

brains are artificially intelligent super

learning computers nicknamed non-binary.

These computer brains were designed by

some wealthy guy known as Sir-Tweets-

A-Lot. Our species are so hard to kill

thanks to regenerative abilities encoded in

our DNA. Anyone who gets in the way of

the rainbow persuasion will meet their god

in Super Hell. Our leader Princess

Tiffanie, will be brought back to life by us

and lead our kind into battle."

The Deadly Switchers had several groups

and hit squads all over the earth hiding in

plain sight and waiting for the war signal.

These Deadly Switchers ran rainbow sex

slave clubs all over the world and they

were their main source of income. The

Deadly Switchers kidnapped thousands of humans worldwide and converted them over to their gender-bender rainbow persuasion. The ORACLE leader finally discovered their master plans by this chance meeting.

The leader of the ORACLE heard enough of this Deadly Switcher nonsense, and she froze time with an app on her phone. The leader silently pulled out a sharp dagger and beheaded the degenerate informant.

Since time was not on, nobody noticed the
ORACLE leader kill this idiot and slipped
out of the hotel unnoticed.

Lord Alexander was enjoying the
company of his newly turned bride Nicole
McBride and his ginger assistants. They
were getting ready for a nightly orgy when
his butler interrupted them. William
barged into the King's chambers and said
that a representative from the ORACLE
was there to see him. The vampire walked

into the King's bedroom and said, "My lord, Princess Tiffanie has been resurrected from the dead by Zarah Jackson! This impure creature is alive and well thanks to Zarah's sorcery! Princess Tiffanie is inside the Esplanade Mansion, and she went on a murderous rampage killing the remnants of the Bally cultists. Princess Tiffanie choked twenty dwarves to death her giant horse leg hanging out its dress and drained their blood dry."

The King gave the immortal from ORACLE five blue magic mushrooms to calm his anxiety and stress. Lord Alexander at once dressed in his favorite Canali suit and ordered his immortal subjects to do the same. Lord Alexander ordered everyone to search the Mansion grounds for Princess Tiffanie so he could kill that bitch again. The King was drunk off the juices of his illustrious sex life when he summoned Kreaper to the war room on the third floor.

Lord Alexander beckoned Kreaper and said, "Kreaper, secure the perimeter and nobody gets in or out of this bitch! You need to find out where B, P, and C went. I cannot believe we do not know where A and R are at either! Did you catch all that, Kreaper?" Kreaper laughed and responded, "Sir, with all due respect, the only thing I learned from your drunkard mouth was the fucking alphabet!"

The King's butler, William, explained the

situation to Kreaper in detail. Kreaper now

understood the magnitude of the

circumstances inside the Esplanade

Mansion. Kreaper summoned the Elite

Daytime Guardians to hunt the Deadly

Switcher down by any means necessary.

The two teams and gingers searched

everywhere for Princess Tiffanie, Saul,

and Zarah Jackson. The enemies were

nowhere to be found inside the Mansion

and had vanished without a trace. Kreaper and Mary gave their reports to the King of New Orleans. The information went in one ear and slid out the other.

The King's ginger assistants threw the drained bodies of the Bally cultists into the bayou for Sampson and his gator children to eat. Lord Alexander resumed plowing and fertilizing Nicole McBride's lady garden and did not care that his enemies disappeared. Nicole McBride sucked the

King dry and a knock on the door

interrupted them. It was William

informing the King that Mr. Porsche was

stolen by Zarah Jackson, Princess Tiffanie,

and Saul.

Lord Alexander ordered every vampire

wise guy and gal in New Orleans to hunt

them down. The King put the word out

that the three thieves were to be executed

on the spot if his Porsche was found in

Zarah's possession. Lord Alexander

ordered Dawn Lightfoot to curse Zarah's

family with her voodoo powder to make

them dazed and confused. Dawn Lightfoot

sprinkled the goofer dust all around

Zarah's home and said, "This wretched

family will die within seven days before

the next full moon." Dawn Lightfoot

walked backwards three steps and turned

around to leave. She repeated the curse

three times and spit on their doorstep as is

custom with voodoo death curses.

The King had strong feelings of love for Zarah but knew she must be eliminated from the earth. Zarah Jackson and 'grabbing balls' Saul snorted three lines of cocaine in the Porsche and Saul beat his meat in the backseat. Saul sprayed the back seat with his dwarven man spunk and stained the leather. Suppose Lord Alexander found that little cocksucker he would have him thrown into a cobra pit to fight for his freedom.

Zarah Jackson was all coked up and having flashbacks from dating Lord Alexander. She recalled a story from long ago in which she invited the King to her Mardi Gras party. Zarah stopped the world time, and the earth froze still. Lord Alexander as a human in his twenties ate Zarah's homemade king cake and found the slice with the king cake baby hidden inside. Lord Alexander lied to Zarah and her mother Mildred and said he did not receive the baby in his slice. Receiving the baby meant the person would receive vast fortune in life and would have to buy the

next king cake the following Mardi Gras

and marry the hostess if she were

unmarried.

Lord Alexander was broker than two

jokers and said he did not know who

received the king cake baby. Thanks to

Lord Alexander's bold lie, Zarah and her

family were cursed by king cake baby

demon living in hell. Zarah became a

drunken and lecherous baby maker, her

mother lost her high paying job, Zarah's father had multiple heart attacks, strokes, and her children were all born with autism.

The king cake baby demon blessed Lord Alexander and he made a fortune in his lumberjack business for ten years. The king cake baby demon also changed Lord Alexander's fate with a flick of his wand. That is how Lord Alexander crossed paths with Lord Baar and became cursed to live as a vampire for eternity. The original path

Lord Alexander was supposed to have been Zarah's hand in marriage. Zarah and her stupid pink hair plagued New Orleans as she sought revenge years later. The curse of Lord Alexander and Zarah Jackson led to New Orleans descending into never ending chaos.

The King also placed a secret voodoo vampire curse on the New Orleans police department, and they disbanded seven months later. A bitch police officer named

Linda Marco, called him a gangster and it took only one insult to incur Lord Alexander's wrath. Linda Marco also stole the King's flowers from his garden, and he hung Linda Marco with piano wire from a streetlight to send a message to the rest of the corrupt police throughout Louisiana.

Lord Alexander offered Zarah and her autistic children the entire west wing of the Esplanade Mansion as penance for cursing her family. Zarah Jackson refused

the King's offer out of pride, and she
whored her way around Louisiana and
Mexico.

Zarah Elizabeth Jackson was gifted the
Boozy and Floozy Witch bar by Lord
Alexander. That was the only present
Zarah would accept since it fueled her
cocaine and alcohol addiction. Zarah was
ungrateful and hated Lord Alexander most
of the time as she never forgave him for
the curse her family had to endure.

Zarah told Princess and Saul that she rarely loved Lord Alexander and only used Lord Alexander to lubricate her dry throat with his special white sauce. Lord Alexander resented Zarah Jackson since she fucked all of his friends, including his male best friend, Bobby Johnson.

Zarah used every man for their sperm to spread her unholy seed all over the French Quarter. Zarah Jackson was such a floozy and she helped herself to every woman's husband or boyfriend. Zarah also stole wives and girlfriends too since she was of the tri-sexual persuasion. Zarah fucked her way throughout the United States and even slept with a few US Presidents. Zarah swindled everyone she dated and stole their credit cards to fund her Amazon Prime shopping sprees. Zarah created her purple crystal wand out of nothing and empowered it with lava from a Hawaiian volcano.

Zarah Jackson also had the ability to

manipulate time and reality around here.

Nobody, not even the reigning Voodoo

Queen of New Orleans or the Great

Sorcerer Lou, were powerful enough to

stop her drunken agenda.

A SCALE OF THIS MAGNITUDE

Fast forward to present day and Princess
Tiffanie had something to say to Zarah
Jackson: "Zarah, you may be all right in
my book since we both hate Lord
Alexander with a passion. Zarah, you
loved the King sometimes and he cursed

your family after you rejected his love.

You and I should join forces and kill the

vampire King of New Orleans finally!"

Zarah Jackson loved the idea of killing

Lord Alexander and anyone associated

with his kingdom. Zarah had a secret she

did not want the world to know. This

hidden truth was the real source of her

power and ability to control everything.

Big Gay Salazar approached the

Esplanade Mansion and knocked on the

front entrance door. He had bricks full of

his Past, Present, and Future weed. Big

Gay Salazar pushed the intercom button

and shouted, "Hey kids, does anybody

want to buy or smoke drugs? I have my

famous fortune teller weed and a new

strain I harvested last Friday." Lord

Alexander remembered how frightening

Big Gay Salazar's fortune teller herb was

when he smoked that shit. The King

needed to get stoned again since the

dynamic boozy and floozy witch, was on

the loose trying to kill him. Lord

Alexander said, "Big Gay Sal, every time we smoke your weed something terrible happens, man. I like the drugs you grow but you need to tone that shit down. It is way too strong for a herculean vampire like me. I guess we should smoke our brains out and I hope I do not travel back to the past this time. You see, I have top-secret mafia business that must be conducted in New Orleans soon."

Big Gay Salazar pulled out a leather

satchel and inside it was a shiny glowing

red bong. Big Gay Salazar told the King,

"You can thank your accountant Ka-Ching

for having me here tonight. I flew over to

the

Esplanade Mansion on my Hoover

vacuum cleaner since my fat ass broke my

broom again. Ka-Ching paid for all this

weed with your American Express black

card. I hope that you do not mind that this

shit right here costed you enough gold to

fund a poor children's orphanage for a year."

Queen Nicole McBride said, "I hope you are joking you, fat bastard! I already used my husbands credit card and bought this gorgeous 2024 Porsche 911 Turbo S." The King exclaimed, "everyone spends daddy bat's money and you guys are a bunch of irresponsible pieces of shit! I am trying to save money and invest, and you people are spending my gold on frivolous bullshit to

tickle your pickles."

Big Gay Salazar said, "Lord Alexander,

you may be the rightful King of New

Orleans! You should shut the fuck up and

smoke this dank ass herb you paid for.

You have more money than the Catholic

Church, stop whining!" Big Gay Salazar

pulled out his new strain called Dragon's

Breath and everyone inside the Mansion

got higher than three nailed Christs sitting

on a misty mountain top.

Lord Alexander in his stoned state of mind

raised the glowing bong to the heavens

and said, "All of you take this dank ass

weed and smoke of it. This stank ass herb

died for your immortal sins. Smoke this

Dragon's Breath in memory of me!"

The reality bending super bong was forged

in Big Gay Salazar's bed with his big

scary feet. A stoned Salazar blessed the pipe to give the cleanest bong rips known to science fiction. The glass pipe was a metaphor not to fuck with the occult or drugs.

The Esplanade Mansion's inhabitants smoked the shit out of that Dragon's Breath, and everyone began hallucinating from the THC. Two fire breathing dragons appeared out of nowhere and slammed into the side of the building. The dragons spit fireballs at the front entrance, and it created a massive whole for them to fly in and cause chaos.

Zarah Jackson appeared out of nowhere riding one of the dragons. Lord Alexander said, "Looks like the wicked bitch of the southwest is here to do battle with me. Everyone I want you to observe America's 'favorite' harlot riding a dragon to kill the King of New Orleans."

Zarah Jackson said, "Lord Alexander you have no idea what you signed up for when you moved to this city ages ago. You see, I am the Past, Present, and Future. I am the Alpha and the Omega. I am the builder and destroyer of universes. I am your Judgement and your Curse. I am the decider of fate and the god of everything that oversees all creation. I am here to adjudicate you for your blasphemous sins against humanity. It is I who decides life and death."

The King, Queen and gingers prepared for the fight of their lives. They had no idea that Zarah Jackson was the god of everything. The vampires thought she was just a drunken, baby making, crackwhore that got a hold of the wrong shit. Zarah waved her left hand and summoned both angels and demons from an alternate reality.

Zarah continued her speech: "I AM THE VIRUS AND THE CURE! I WILL DESTROY THIS PLANET AND EVERY LIVING BEING THROUGHOUT THE UNIVERSE. YOU VAMPIRES THOUGHT I WAS JUST A CRACK WHORE THAT PLAYED GOD. I AM ACTUALLY GOD AND YOU ALL WILL DIE TONIGHT! I AM EVERYTHING AND NOTHING. I AM HOPE AND DESPAIR."

With a wave of her wand, Drunk Zarah, killed one hundred citizens inside the Esplanade Mansion. She sent the angels and demons to terrorize Lord Alexander and his friends. Everyone fought back and scores of the Esplanade Mansion's inhabitants were killed with brute force. Lord Alexander was scared for the first time in his immortal life. Lord Alexander and Lady Nicole appeared no match for THE GOD OF EVERYTHING.

Zarah and her gangster terrorist followers
swarmed every room inside the building
killing off anyone that resisted. Zarah
demanded worship and praise by the
people or would cut off their heads with
her razor-sharp stiletto heels if they
refused.

The King and Queen of New Orleans
killed the dragon Princess Tiffanie was
riding on that night. The vampires
summoned their mystical silver swords

and killed dozens of Zarah's gangster terrorists as possible. The angels and demon terrorists were no match for the might and power of the immortals.

The God of Everything grew impatient with the onslaught. Instead of wishing the vampires out of existence with her wand she kidnapped Queen Nicole and vanished. Lord Alexander became distraught at losing his queen and the gingers consoled him. Zarah and her gangster terrorists vanished without a trace

leaving the kingdom without a queen.

Dawn Lightfoot appeared and restored the

busted-up building back to normal with a

voodoo spell she learned in the third

grade. Dawn Lightfoot pulled out her

wand and hypnotized Lord Alexander to

ease his mental anguish. She

reprogrammed the King to find a new

queen to ease his sorrowful heart.

Lord Alexander asked for fresh blood to recuperate from the large battle. William brought him a goblet and a hot woman called the Mad Doctor. The King grew infatuated with this Mad Doctor woman since she was five times hotter than Nikki and Sam Jordan combined.

The Mad Doctor and King of New Orleans hit thing off super well. They had an intense relationship that centered on the most powerful sex on the earth. The Mad

Doctor introduced Lord Alexander to the

most incredible wettest and tightest vagina

know to mankind. They had the most

wonderful sex five times a day and they

married after only knowing each other for

a month.

The new queen, The Mad Doctor had a

way of controlling the King with her

gaslighting techniques she learned in PSY

Ops. She also used her magical pussy to

control the King to do her financial

bidding and taxes too. The King feared this Mad Doctor psychologically and she knew it too. He tried to break up their marriage three times and she tried to have him assassinated by her gangster friends from Boston.

No matter how many times the Mad Doctor upset him, he could never get enough of the Mad Doctor's godly juices of life covering his face. Lord Alexander was hooked on the Mad Doctor's magical body, tight love maker, and everything about this woman turned him on like a Christmas Tree. The Mad Doctor treated her husband like her therapist because she had demons from her past that haunted her in the military.

Their personalities often clashed and there was a constant power struggle between the two. The Mad Doctor wished to control everything the King did, and he resented her for it. The Mad Doctor hired one of her old boyfriends to kill the King after he

refused to buy her super expensive

jewelry. The King was on his way to a

meeting with the King of New York City

when a special bullet ricocheted off Mr.

Porsche's windshield. The Mad Doctor

pretended to play dumb and downplayed

the incident as an imagination by the King.

The Mad Doctor never apologized for

gaslighting her husband since she believed

she was always right. The Mad Doctor did

not care that she destroyed the King on a

daily basis, and she got off on the pain she

caused him. The only thing the King and

Queen had in common was an insatiable

appetite for mind blowing sex that would

make Satan envious.

Lord Alexander became disillusioned with

this Mad Doctor from hell. He felt the

only way they could get past the

arguments would be turn her into a

vampire. Senorita Psychopath happily

became one and used her immortal power to forge gangster friendships and secret lovers behind the King's back.

The King of New Orleans had thousands of human and vampire lovers throughout his life, and he knew they were expendable and replaceable.

The King would help their human son, Damien build puzzles and Lego sets. Damien love bombed the King every day and the King was delighted that this human child was so affectionate and a happy little boy.

The Mad Doctor praised the King to his face and lied behind his back to her Muslim friend. The Mad Doctor and her Muslim friend were secretly lovers and they plotted to destroy the King of New Orleans in order to seize control over the city.

The Muslim hated Lord Alexander with a passion and would call him a narcissistic prick behind his back. The King hated this bitch because she filled the Mad Doctor's mind full of poisonous lies and accused the King of cheating on the Mad Doctor.

One day Lord Alexander had enough of this Muslim scum and had her thrown into a lake of fire by the Elite Daytime Guardians. Kreaper kidnapped this bitch in the middle of the night and stabbed her repeatedly in the stomach to prolong her suffering and to murder the bitch. Lord Alexander pissed on the Muslim's head and placed it atop a necromancer staff and gave it to the Great Sorcerer Lou for his fealty.

THE HIDDEN TEMPLE AND ZARAH'S POWER

The Vampire God Vincent took a vacation from killing Deadly Switchers since he only got two inches of sleep a day. He flew to the Thar Desert and buried himself deep in the beige sand so he could dream about killing pepperoni. Vincent was almost asleep when a weird looking yogi woke him up.

The desert yogi told Vincent, "Vampire

God when you have a bad day, fuck it!

Just give up and go home to your hookers.

Fuck it all! You are not going to die in this

Thar Desert. You are not rock and are the

golden wind. I will show you the way to

paradise."

Vincent was furious with this crackpot

Indian yogi for interrupting his two inches

of sleep. Vincent said, "Yogi crackhead, I

am trying to rest up before I find the

temple to help me in my quest. Piss off before I drain you dry and wear your face as a Halloween mask!" The yogi laughed and vanished before Vincent's eyes. The yogi reappeared behind the vampire god and said, "Ah death, is it? Death is my friend, and it should be yours too. If what you are living for is not worth dying for, then find different purpose in life. I will take you to the temple you seek. I first must evaluate you to see if you are ready for what is to come. The real reason you never sleep more than two inches a day is because you have the curse of the vampire

god bestowed upon you by the god of

everything."

Vincent was unsure of what to make of

this Indian yogi. He turned around to grab

him by the yogi's throat, but it was

Vincent's throat grabbed instead. The yogi

flipped the vampire god on his back using

his right hand. The yogi held him down

and repeatedly slapped Vincent in the face

until his blood was everywhere.

The yogi pulled out a flute and put Vincent under a trance. He made the vampire god wander the desert for five nights without a drop of blood. The thirst hit Vincent like a ton of bricks, and he tried to bite the yogi on the neck multiple times. The yogi dodged every attack from Vincent and soon Vincent felt death approaching his prehistoric carcass.

Vincent's strong will broke through the

trance occasionally and he asked where

the hidden temple was at in the desert. The

yogi used his flute and played an

intoxicating song for the vampire god.

Vincent began hallucinating and started to

speak in his original language to the yogi.

The yogi silenced him, and Vincent

imagined Super Satan was ripping him

apart limb from limb. The boozy and

floozy witch, also known as the god of

everything appeared in the sky.

Zarah mocked the vampire god from the clouds, and he fell from the blood thirst. The yogi knew Vincent would expire soon without blood and he offered his wrist to the immortal. Vincent grabbed the yogi's forearm with herculean strength and nearly drained the yogi dry. The Indian man slapped Vincent with his back left hand, and he regenerated his blood quickly. Vincent speculated under this yogi's flute influence that Zarah was actually the god of everything and not some made up science fiction bullshit.

The yogi taught Vincent that Zarah predated time itself and only pretended to be human to blend in with her creation. The yogi told Vincent the only way to defeat the god of everything was through going through a difficult trial inside the Temple of Sex and Pain.

Vincent kept having visions of Zarah and they appeared both real and fantasy at the same time. Zarah would get bored with history and rewrite it for her own amusement. The god of everything controlled the yogi briefly and made him tell Vincent that he was going to be wiped from reality by her. How odd that the god of everything was a drunken lush that chose New Orleans to put her spell bound baby maker to clever use. Zarah was one piece of work. She was fully divine and fully human. She was both God and Satan.

Friend and Foe.

Zarah constantly rewrote reality to confuse the vampire god and Vincent was shown numerous versions of himself. In one reality he was married to Zarah, and they had six children. In the other reality he was her underground basement sex slave. In the third reality he was shown to be only a mortal zookeeper without enough money to fuel his Nissan 350 Z.

Lord Vincent began to question his own sanity as his thoughts were manipulated and twisted by the god of everything for her sadistic pleasure. Lord Vincent could not remember when he came into being the vampire god. Was it one hundred thousand years ago or was it last week? He began to doubt his ability to fight off the reality bending from the god of everything.

He tried to breathe and free his mind from Zarah's mental prison. Lord Vincent began to pull his hair out in frustration since Zarah was deep inside his mind and tormenting him. The yogi laughed as Vincent cried out in mental anguish and Vincent begged for the god of everything to kill him.

Yogi Jimi woke the vampire god from his intoxicating trance and vanished without a trace. The Temple of Sex and Pain appeared before Vincent's eyes. Vincent

wandered the Thar desert for over forty

years and not a couple of weeks like he

thought. Lord Vincent developed more

combat prowess thanks to Yogi Jimi

manipulating his DNA with his magic

flute. Yogi Jimi trained Vincent in desert

god hand-to-hand combat. Lord Vincent's

body and mind moved more independently

of each other after these training sessions.

Vincent grew faster and more robust than

ever before in his lifetime.

Vincent started to appreciate that since he was a vampire god, he was both alive and dead at the same time. Before Lord Vincent could open the entrance to the temple, Zarah stopped him in his tracks. The god of everything whispered in Vincent's ear that it was too late to stop her.

Yogi Jimi reappeared behind Vincent and offered to train him one last time before going into the temple. Yogi Jimi fucked up Vincent's world and introduced Vincent to triple light speed striking. Vincent's eyes could not see Yogi Jimi's hands and feet striking him. He was convinced this Yogi Jimi was in his imagination and not real. Lord Vincent asked him, "How in the fucking fuck are you so dynamic in combat? I have been alive longer than this desert and I have never met anyone of your caliber in a fight!"

Yogi Jimi replied, "Are you sure this is reality? Am I real? Are you real or imaginary like Jesus? Do you think you can hit me?" Lord Vincent let go all thoughts of reality and fantasy and completely emptied his mind. He did not focus on fighting anymore and instead imagined retiring on the moon. Yogi Jimi unleashed a furious relentless assault on the Vampire God and was beaten stupid.

Vincent was gifted more of the yogi's blood to prevent the thirst from ravaging his old body. Vincent had enough strength from the battle, and he kicked the yogi in the throat and knocked him out cold. Vincent drained the yogi dry, and the yogi's body faded into the sand. Vincent was happy to kill this Desert Jesus looking fellow.

Vampire God Vincent heard that Zarah was the Original God of Everything from a demon he tortured a thousand years ago.

Who would have guessed a baby making

slut would be hiding in plain sight in New

Orleans? The only way to discover this

truth is to enter the temple and find the

truthful answer.

In front of the entrance to the temple was a

drunk male cat reading and two kittens in

his lap. Vampire God Vincent was

humored by this drunk cat reading stories

to two little kittens. Vincent approached

the cats and petted them. He asked, "What are you doing in this scorching desert by yourselves? It is too hot out and you are drinking whiskey in this forsaken heat! Your kittens will perish without water or milk. What are you thinking???" The older bearded cat answered him in English, "I am thinking about murder! Cats always think about murder, which is what makes us more dangerous than dogs. We are crafty and sneaky motherfuckers compared to those stupid canines. Are you shocked I am talking Vampire God?"

Lord Vincent replied, "Either I see a mirage, or this littler fucker is talking to me right now! How in Satan's black beard are you speaking right now? There is no way you are from earth! Cats do not talk unless I missed the memo. What is your name you cute furry little fucker?"

The cat replied, "I am George the talking cat and I am from purgatory. The god of everything created me by mistake and left me to rot in purgatory. I knew she was a

boozed out drunken lush whore and would

pass out from the angelic wine I brewed. I

escaped from purgatory by slipping

through a portal to the earth. Two angels

were guarding the portal and I threw some

weed and whiskey on the ground and

watched the two guardians fight over it.

As they beat the holy hell out of each

other I slipped by jumped in the portal and

landed in this ungodly hot desert. My balls

here are melting in the sand and who

shows up here? The Vampire God that I

have admired from above since I was first

breathed into existence by that drunken

harlot Zarah. I have always wanted to

meet a Vampire God in person and here

we are today. I got busy with Ms. Kitty

and have all these kittens to feed. That is

why you should stick with Jack Daniels

and not that Fireball booty hole shit!"

Lord Vincent grew more fascinated with

this angry talking kitty. They laughed and

laughed outside the temple and the

Vampire God forgot about his mission briefly as he found a new best friend in the desert. Lord Vincent caught three sand vipers and ripped their heads off to feed his new furry best friend and his little kitty children. George the talking cat told Vincent that since he was given Yogi Jimi's blood that he now had the ability to communicate with all animals and sea creatures on the planet.

The Vampire told the cat, "There must

some freaky desert voodoo in that old

Yogi's blood!" George stroked his beard

and replied, "Yeah, that motherfucker!

Yogi Jimi has potent desert ass voodoo

coursing balls deep inside his veins. That

is how he beat your stupid ass multiple

times in combat. He is the god of the Thar

Desert, and he assesses all travelers that

lose their way in the desert. He likes to kill

people he feels is not worthy of his

teachings. The only reason he would not

kill you was because you reminded him of

his father, and he could not bring himself to destroying your immortal ass. You look almost identical to Yogi Jimi's father the god of the Mohave Desert, Carl. Another reason Yogi Jimi was able to whip your ass in combat so efficiently is the Thar Desert is far older than you imagined it to be. The Thar Desert was imported by the god of everything from hell, and it predates the earth itself. Yogi Jimi was a fallen angel who fell with Lucifer and his rebellious brethren. His angel's name was Samael, and he became Yogi Jimi after losing a poker card game to Lucifer three times in a row. Lucifer gave him the power over the Thar Desert and made him a god of these sands. The people of India worshipped Yogi Jimi as the leader of the Hindu gods. Yogi Jimi blessed the Indian people with peace and prosperity until an Arabian man, Aladdin stole his bitch and kissed her apples."

Lord Vincent was fascinated with history, and he knew this talking cat was really intelligent despite being a drunkard desert bum. Lord Vincent remembered his mission to infiltrate the Temple of Sex and Pain. He was having too much fun despite the god of everything appearing as a face on the moon threatening to wipe all existence and reality. Lord Vincent stole George's Jack Daniels and Cuban cigars and went to town on the free shit. George was irritated, but there was not much he could do to get his drink and tobacco back from the Vampire God. Lord Vincent drank the shit out of that Jack Daniels, and he slap boxed the cat for fun. Lord

Vincent kept control over his potent

strength, and it was a fun game for the cat

too. George the cat pulled out a long

wooden pipe from his Air Jordan

backpack, hit that pipe, and blew a large

ring of blue opium smoke in Lord

Vincents face. The second-hand blue

smoke cloud smacked Vincent's mind

back to the ancient Roman Empire and he

tripped his ass off.

Zarah's invisible body appeared next to

Lord Vincent and George the talking cat.

She whispered in Lord Vincents ear, "You

are a failure, you are nothing and you will

fail your mission. I am amused you think a

mere vampire god can defeat the god of

everything. I transcend reality, time, and

the universe. I created you and I can

destroy you. Give up! I only allow

vampires to exist so they can depopulate

the earth from time to time. It is less work

I have to do with great floods, plagues,

and wars. I am not to be trifled with by the

likes of you. I am a baby making machine

and that Christ fellow did not die for your

sins. He died for mine. It was a sin to

create humanity, the vampire race and

anything else breathing oxygen. I caused

that virgin to be pregnant by entering her

lady box and my Spirit went to town on

that little Jewish bitch's love box. The

belief that a cosmic Jewish carpenter

zombie was his own father and if you

telepathically tell him he is your master.

You will live forever because a rib

woman, named Eve, ate sinful fruit, and

had sex with a talking snake. Makes

perfect sense!" The god of everything had

a strange dark sense of humor.

Lord Vincent knew this unstable god of

everything had to go away. This

psychopathic bitch would destroy

everything including herself if that is what

it took to make all matter cease to exist.

Zarah was a miserable drunkard god that

hated herself and punished the universe for

it. No one was close to being on an equal

level with her except her first husband, the god of chaos and destruction, Javiel.

George the cat, led Vampire God Vincent to the temple entrance and they were still higher than three kites. They saw strange three-legged flamingoes flying over their heads. Lord Vincent was disoriented from the opium, and he was drowsy too. He said to the cat, "George I am so tired that I could fall asleep right outside this temple until the cash me outside girl is old enough to be President of the United States. I am so high from that dancing devil opium that I predict I will be the last straight male on earth. I see purple and black snakes crawling out of our brains and I am glad I can count to potato right now." They laughed their asses off as the dancing devil opium took over their minds.

Lord Vincent and George, the cat nodded off and fell asleep listening to the sand blowing in the wind. They slept for a week straight and George's ex wife Melinda took George's kittens home to safety.

The door to the Temple of Sex and Pain was locked from the outside with a magic seal and it stood thirty feet tall. The entrance was made of solid gold, and it was adorned with chaos magic sigils protecting it from intruders. The temple itself was a thousand feet tall and the peak surrounded by colorful clouds and a red aura.

Lord Vincent and George, the cat woke up

from their drug fueled slumber and George

was in a panic since his kittens were

missing in action. He called his ex-wife

Melinda on the phone and shouted,

"Where are my kittens, bitch? Daddy

misses his children!" Melinda said, "While

you were too busy getting white girl

wasted with the Vampire God, I took them

to my house so they would not starve to

death. You had been passed out cold from

smoking that opium shit for a week

straight. You are one lazy and

irresponsible parent and should be

ashamed of yourself, George! You and

your little ass dick are the reason I

divorced you in cat court and took all the

money. I will see to it you pay me more in

kitten support you slimy furball!"

Lord Vincent told George, "Fuck your ex-

wife we have to save the world from the

god of everything and time is running

out." George told the Vampire God,

"Suppose you have been married five

times like I have. You qualify for hell's
employment program. You get to be a tour
guide in hell since torturing the soul is no
surprise after being married and divorced
five time. You get to help Satan torture the
unwed mother's club of debauchery.
Torture is no surprise if you have been
married. Satan cannot scare the fuck out of
those that were wed and tortured by their
spouses! You will even develop a super
primal scream like goddamn Sam Kinison
after you have been in love nine times."

George, the cat, told Lord Vincent he can open the temple by thinking of a gorgeous woman and taking away reason and accountability. That did not work, and they were back to square one in figuring out the way inside the beautiful temple. Lord Vincent called Lord Alexander and asked him to send the Great Sorcerer Lou to open the temple since prehistoric chaos magic was his specialty.

The Great Lou was in the middle of getting his dick sucked by somebody's wife and had no choice but to help the Vampire God. Lord Alexander threatened him with imprisonment should he refuse the vampire mafia don's request.

The Great Lou showed up on his flying vacuum cleaner with his magical chaos staff adorned with the head of the Muslim chick. He pointed the staff at the gold door and said, "Guess what motherfucker, I am the Great Sorcerer Lou, and I command you to open this bitch up or I will blast you with enough chaos energy to incinerate this temple and burn this motherfucker to the ground!" The temple entrance flung wide open as the chaos energy manipulated the magic seal and it obeyed the sorcerer. The Great Lou went back to New York city since he had a married woman to fertilize with his potent seed of life.

Inside the main entrance were these gorgeous thirty-foot-tall triple breasted demon babes hailing from the Abyss. They came in all assorted colors and were sucking vampire golf balls through their garden hoses! One of the gorgeous she-demons said to Lord Vincent, "Welcome to Super Hell! The Temple of Sex and Pain is where you will learn the ways of intense pleasure, finances, and of course pain behind comprehension!"

Lord Vincent thought about what this hot

demon said to him and was both intrigued

and confused. He thought he was going to

just get his prick sucked and learn how to

defeat the god of everything and her true

power. Lord Vincent said, "Yeah, those

ladies! What in the hell am I going to learn

from pleasure, pain, and finances? How

can I learn to manage my money if you

lady demons are too busy blowing my

balls into oblivion?" The god of

everything was invisible but could be

heard cackling like a crack whore in the

background. Zarah observed the Vampire God and talking cat falling right into her well-placed trap.

Zarah chilled the room to where the nipples would be stiffer than a porn star. Zarah telepathically instructed the demon women to strap Lord Vincent to a wood framed bed and torture him to death. She said the same thing about George the talking cat.

Lord Vincent saw the demon babes

approaching him with whips and silver

straps. He said, "Yippie I am getting

strapped, whipped, and fucked like

nobody's business!" The demons whipped

the shit out of Lord Vincent to the point he

cried out in pain. These demon whores hit

harder than Mike Tyson beating up a

broke drug dealer hopped up on PCP.

Lord Vincent tried to fight back since he

did not like how hard they were cracking

the whips on his body. The demons surrounded the vampire god and two of them grabbed his arms and dragged him to a bed found at the top of the temple.

The demon Morgos ordered George the cat whipped unmercifully by the giant demon babes. George the cat was beaten stupid by the giants, and he became delirious from the incredible pain. He spoke to them and said, "Wow these whips just tickle my little furry balls! Beat me harder mommy!" The demons did as was ordered of them and beat the cat unconscious.

The demon Shelo hopped on Lord Vincent's massive member, and he blew his golden nut all over the place. Shelo slapped him for finishing too early and Lord Vincent spat in her face. Shelo grabbed a pair of silver pliers and squeezed Lord Vincent's fingers and broke them one by one. Lord Vincent tried to telepathically summon Lord Alexander for help, but the temple's chaos magic prevented any thoughts from Lord Vincent being transmitted outside its walls.

The demons beat the dynamic duo increasingly. Until they longed for a swift death. As the demons beat the two best friends up, they taught them how to balance a checkbook, invest in the stock market and how to hide from any money hungry baby mommas.

Shelo and Toras whipped out a chalkboard and educated them on how to do their own taxes and log in receipts into a ledger. George the cat said, "Bitch, what the hell is a ledger and I never do my own taxes since I am known as the tax evasion king from purgatory!" The demon babes put a yellow ball gag in Geroge's mouth, and he mumbled under his breath how he hated talking about money. His ex-wife Melinda got 85% of his income through an illegal kitten support order in a kickback deal with the supreme court cat family judge, Shirley Templeton.

Lord Vincent was gagged with pink demon panties with silver wrapped around to burn his ashen colored skin. He got high off the lovely scent and the demons beat him some more for trying to talk. Gorgana ordered Lord Vincent to be silent and pleasure her sexy clitoris with his pointy pale nose. Lord Vincent nosed Gorgana's wet clitoris by using the alphabet, A, B, C,

D, etc. Lord Vincent was enjoying the

scent of her fertile honey flavored love

garden.

Gorgana beat Lord Vincent until he passed

out from the pain after he refused to go

any faster on her love button between her

legs. Lord Vincent was trying to enjoy the

heavenly scent and savor it in the back of

his throat. Gorgana ordered the Vampire

God to be damaged higher with stage two

pain. Seven demons appeared from a portal and unleashed a furious dagger assault on his stomach.

The seven demons stabbed him repeatedly and Lord Vincent realized he really was in Super Hell. Nobody was able to hear his cries for help or his begging for mercy. The triple breasted demons ungagged the Vampire God and they each took turns sitting on his ancient face. Lord Vincent was ordered by Gorgana, to lick their

pussies until it felt like his long tongue
was about to fall off. He could not enjoy
their nectar with his mouth because of the
insane amount of blood loss and pain.
Lord Vincent cried out for the demons to
kill him, but they refused.

Lord Vincent was infuriated that he was
trapped by these demon whores from hell
and wondered who was behind the
madness, besides Zarah. He yelled out, "I
am the Vampire God, it should be me

doing the fucking. I do not get fucked."

Shelo silenced him with a punch to the

face and ordered him to suck the honey

flavored milk from her succulent breasts.

Immediately the milk hit Lord Vincent

like a ton of bricks, and he began

hallucinating. He saw three Zarah's

laughing at him at the foot of the fifty-

foot-long bed.

Lord Vincent saw a vision of Zarah in

which she truly was the god of everything

and predated time itself. Lord Vincent

realized New Orleans and the universe

were completely fucked if the god of

everything went through with her plans of

destroying everything including herself.

He also saw a vison in which every living

being retired Zarah's sexual jersey at least

twice on Mondays.

Two demons with pink hair and purple

bodies appeared from the ceiling and

dropped down below. They wrote on a

board on how to pay and receive money with an artificially intelligent wallet app. The vampire god jerked his chicken with his free arm and asked, "What does this artificial intelligent wallet have to do with defeating the god of everything?" The demon known as Mobaduk, stuck her pretty painted toes in his mouth to get him to shut the fuck up.

Lord Alexander's accountant Ka-Ching appeared inside the top floor torture room riding a massive spider. Ka-Ching said to Lord Vincent, "You may be the vampire god of this planet, but I am the god of this temple in another dimension. I have been eagerly waiting to kill you off since you first created me three thousand years ago. You see ole Vinny, I wish to take your place as the god of the earth. Lord Vincent you are the first of our kind and yet not the most intelligent. I made a deal with Zarah to lure you here. George the cat being tortured was a bonus. You wish to know how to defeat the god of everything, right?

Guess what motherfucker? Zarah cannot be defeated period. Her power is beyond our wildest dreams and imagination. Just imagine the Christian God and Satan fusing together into one primordial being. That still would not explain the vast knowledge and strength she has in the universe. She is both real and science fiction. Zarah's ability to manipulate time and reality cannot be stopped by you or Lord Alexander. You wasted your time and fell directly into our trap. I will gladly drain all your blood and become God and

Satan of the earth."

Ka-Ching began choking the life out of

Lord Vincent with both hands in a fit of

rage. He then ripped a sharp stiletto off

Shelo's heel and stabbed him in the throat.

Lord Vincent was at the brink of death and

his gold aura began to fade as the blood

squirted all over the onyx floor. Lord

Vincent tried to summon Lord Alexander

to save him again, but it failed miserably.

His thoughts only echoed inside his own head, and he felt dread.

More and more triple-breasted demons emerged from purple portals from the Abyss and Abaddon the demon king joined them. Abaddon said, "Get a tombstone and inscribe, 'Here Lies The Gold People, The King of Nothing!' and make sure to beat Lord Vincent in the face with the stone slab." Lord Vincent's thoughts spun in terror as the demons beat him repeatedly in the face with the

tombstone. Lord Vincent embraced the

idea of death and no longer being

immortal. His pain would finally cease

suppose he died today.

Ka-Ching and the demons tortured him

with their magic wands. They shot hell

flames into his face and lightning into his

ball sack. Ka-Ching and Abaddon showed

him no mercy as they poured battery acid

on his feet and covered his shoulders with mosquitoes.

Vampire God Vincent screamed in terror and pure agony as the torture did not seem to let up. Lord Vincent struggled to free himself from the chains and was unsuccessful. Lord Vincent glared at Ka-Ching and said, "You will not get away with murdering the Vampire God and George the cat! Lord Alexander will punish you for your treachery and deceit! I always have a contingency plan and that is what makes me the Godfather of all vampires. You may be the god of this temple and ruler of this dimension. My allegiance runs far beyond these walls. I have an elite group of vampire gangster terrorists that are on the way here. I have a tracking device implanted in my left hand. Soon you will suffer for your poisonous treachery and swallow death. You said Zarah cannot be defeated and transcends time and reality? Every god can be conquered if given enough prep time. I do not care whether Zarah is the god of everything or a moldy can of chicken noodle soup, she can be destroyed! Pay attention Ka-Ching, you will die twice soon. I will find a way to kill off that wretched baby maker, Zarah, and take her place as the god of everything!"

Ka-Ching said, "Lord Vincent, you are crazier than a three-dollar hooker on meth if you think I will allow you to escape my domain!" Vampire

God Vincent said, "I am crazier than a three-dollar bill and that is what my ex-wife Zarah said too!"

George the cat was stabbed with little daggers, and he screamed, "Vinny! Help me! Help me! They are going to kill me! They are going to kill me! I am too high off that opium and cannot see straight. Time is not moving in here at all, man! I got all these little kittens to support. Tell them gangster terrorist friends of yours to hurry their asses up. I am getting cold, and I am starting to see platinum Aztec temples and shit."

Ka-Ching and the demonic women increasingly tortured the two best friends. Abaddon stood over top of them sipping dragon blood out of a black goblet. Ka-Ching said, "Lord Vincent, you will give me your blood, body, and soul to make me like you in power. I want to further my unholy demonic mafia family agenda. You and Lord Alexander are the only immortals standing in my way."

Ka-Ching pulled out a silver dagger from his leather boot and sliced the Vampire God's wrists wide open. Ka-Ching and the triple-breasted demons gorged on his blood and became drunk off his potent blood. God power surged through Ka-Ching and the demons, and they became more robust. They became frenzied versions of themselves and had vampire god strength, speed, and agility. Ka-Ching

and the demons grew lustful with their

new power and beat the holy fuck out of

each other to test it out. Ka-Ching told

Lord Vincent, "I have not felt this alive

since witnessing the construction and

erection of the Statue of Liberty built in

France."

Yogi Jimi's spirit appeared to Lord

Vincent in a vision as his life was fading

into nothing. He said, "When you have a

bad day, fuck it! Go home and take a long nap. Help will arrive soon. Be patient and mindful that every day is not going to be a good day. Some days are just fucked. Your salvation from Ka-Ching will be very soon."

Vampire God Vincent's life was fading faster and faster. He could feel death approaching him and began to embrace the idea of his demise. Lord Vincent was almost empty of his powerful blood, and he longed for execution by the traitorous vampire. Ka-Ching fed him pig blood to prolong his agony and for Ka-Ching's own amusement. Lord Vincent cried out in pain as the monster clamped his feet with a steel torture device.

Ka-Ching told Lord Vincent that he would not be alive much longer. He also told him that he was the salvation of the vampire species, and that Lord Vincent was the virus. Ka-Ching felt he was the cure for

Vampire God Vincent's power over the earth and wanted all his gold and possessions for himself.

Abaddon and the demons danced wildly around the dying vampire. They all took turns spitting on him and mocking him. Ka-Ching said, "Those that want respect from Ka-Ching should give respect." Abaddon's eyes glowed like fire as he pissed on Lord Vincent. George the cat passed out from his own hellish pain.

The god of everything appeared in the flesh and rewarded Ka-Ching for secretly worshipping her and his fealty to her. Zarah was everywhere at once and could channel thoughts from the other side of the universe. She had sex with Ka-Ching and the demons in an orgy to pay Ka-Ching in pussy. Zarah also granted him God of the earth and for all vampire mafia kickbacks to hit his bank account after Lord Vincent perished.

Zarah's power was truly limitless, and she enjoyed toying with her creation every thousand years. Zarah's true nature was fully divine and fully human. She only let vampires exist for her own entertainment. Zarah got off on manipulating worldly affairs, destroying whole nations, and interfering with the vampire mafia. She only pretended to be human because it tickled her clit and made her boobies sing Satanic Hymns.

SEX IN SATANS CHAIR

Zarah grew bored of being the god of

everything and secretly wished the

vampire mafia would find a way to kill her

off for good. She knew the idea of her

death was futile since her power

transcended anything beyond human

comprehension. Zarah had multiple

facades she would show her creation. She

would appear as a mother, grandmother,

child, or schoolteacher.

Zarah created the original immortal

Vincent's spirit out of her magical left

breast and formed his body within the void

of a black hole. Zarah made Lord Vincent

her husband and grew bored with him

since he was not as intelligent or beautiful.

Lord Vincent refused to worship and

praise the god of everything, and it sent

her into a deep-seated depression. Zarah

became unstable and wiped all existence

every thousand years and started over

fresh. The time was almost up for that to

happen again. The vampire mafia was the

only thing that stood in her way. The

people of the earth thought that Jesus

Christ would be their savior and save them

from Zarah. Unfortunately, she created the Christ and the myth surrounding his divinity to take the blame off her failure in creating an imperfect universe. Zarah grew tired of the prayers to God and transformed into the monstrous harlot she is today.

Lord Alexander sent his five gingers to various sex nightclubs throughout New Orleans and New York city to collect 'protection money.' The first bar the gingers stopped was Drunker Than Five Skunks owned by the sleaze ball known as Kevin Beamer. Kevin Beamer was notorious for sleeping with everyone's wife and their sisters. Kevin had no problem ruining peoples' marriages and breaking families apart. Kevin Beamer never believed in foreplay and always went straight for dessert. Kevin was a rich vampire captain in the vampire mafia, and he had the gold to entice women.

The five gingers entered through the back entrance of the bar and saw Kevin snorting cocaine off a stripper's ass in his secret sex toy room. The sex dungeon had all kinds of BDSM equipment, a tall bookshelf full of sex toys and an unorganized amount scattered all over the floor. The gingers rolled their green eyes as Kevin poured expensive whiskey on one of the strippers and licked it off her large breasts.

Kevin paid no attention to the gingers and

beat his meat furiously all over five

strippers inside the sex room. The gingers

appeared silently behind him as he was

getting a blowjob from Cindy Estrada,

who was one of the town whores and

Drunk Donna's sister. Mary said to Kevin,

"Kevin! You really are New Orleans worst

sleaze bag. Cindy is married to the mayor

of New Orleans, and you are in big

trouble. Do you know why we are here a

week early? You missed your vampire

business protection payment, and we are here to collect."

Kevin replied in disgust, "You redheaded ginger bitches are something else. I should not have to keep paying this extortion to the King. He gave me a break this week." Margaret answered, "That is where you are wrong sleaze ball. The Mafia King of New Orleans does not bend the rules, especially for scum like you." Martha chimed in and said, "Suppose you do not want the King to know you are pushing

heroin to high school teens. I suggest you

cough up the ten thousand gold coin right

now and we will not tell him. Heroin is

dirty money, and the King would kill you

if he discovered you were poisoning the

little children of our beautiful city."

Kevin cried bloody tears and said, "Have

mercy on a destitute dirty old man. I have

a sex addiction and selling heroin is how I

pay for that sex. You bitches are some

scary gangster terrorist whores!" Melanie stuck a gun in Kevin's mouth and educated him, "We are the King's whores, and we are not gangsters. We are businesswomen and our business is extorting scumbags like you. Suppose you do not cough up the dough I will paint the walls behind you with your brains and your strippers can watch."

Kevin Beamer began sweating profusely and ordered the two strippers to fetch the gold from the safe in an adjacent room. The strippers brought out ten briefcases totally the ten thousand gold coins and handed it over without incident. Margaret told him that they would be taking his red1969 Mustang GT for his difficult behavior. Kevin swung at Margaret's face with a baseball bat and Mary shot Kevin in the arm with a black assault rifle before he could connect the attack.

Kevin hollered out in pain and cried like a bitch as the gingers stole five bottles of red wine and his Mustang. Melanie grabbed him by the throat and said, "Kevin you are easily replaceable. I could kill you right now if I wanted to do so tonight. I see you chose death instead of cooperating with the King's enforcers. My sisters and I have not tasted vampire in a long time. We will drink your blood, fuck your strippers for free and set you on fire while you are still alive." The gingers slit Kevin's throat with a silver sword, and he stumbled backwards into his black leather couch. The gingers

drank his blood as he writhed in terror.

Kevin was half dead when Mary poured

lighter fluid on him and set his world on

fire. Kevin screamed in agony and burned

to a cremated version of himself.

Agent 0069 Sam Jordan and the Great

Sorcerer Lou showed up after Margaret

phoned them to join their stripper orgy.

Lou had performed a sex magic ritual after

he kissed the head on top of his chaos

staff. He yelled out, "Where them hoes at? I need this big black cock sucked like my vacuum cleaner!" The strippers made the vampires rum punch mixed with fairy blood and they all got higher than shit. Sam Jordan told Lou, "You are lucky the gingers invited you to this orgy. Usually, these sex orgies are an all-female event. I will suck you off first while Margaret and Melanie take turns eating me from the back."

The Great Lou said, "Sweet baby Jesus, I died and went to heaven. I finally got my wish from the sex spell I performed two days ago. Typically, these copulation spells take one full moon cycle to manifest." Sam Jordan replied, "Are you going to keep talking about magic or are you going to start eating our pussies and fucking us with that big black cock? Shut the hell up about moon cycles, sex spells and punish this tight pussy!"

The Great Lou went to town on the
women until he passed out from
exhaustion. He fell asleep in Drunk
Donna's arms and her sister Cindy stole
his Air Jordan Retro 13 shoes and his
wallet. The gingers were still thirsty for
human blood, so they asked Sam Jordan to
drag Lou to her Escalade and drop him off
at home.

Sam Jordan dropped Lou off at his
mansion in the Garden District and she

went home too. The gingers stared down the two strippers with a sadistic smile and said, "Dinner is on me bitches! Gingers drink free!"

The gingers ravaged the strippers, and they screamed uncontrollably as Kevin Beamers hookers were brutally murdered. The five gingers drained both Drunk Donna and Cindy within five minutes. The vampires laughed as the humans' lifeless bodies hit the ground. Mary and Margaret ripped their heads off and danced around the bar with them. Melanie pulled a dildo off the bookshelf and shoved it in Drunk Donna's lifeless head. Melanie said, "Hey Drunk Donna, if you want this fake penis, it will be in my purse or in the refrigerator." Melanie kicked Drunk Donnas head like a soccer ball, and it rolled into the fireplace. Cindy met the same fate as her sister.

The five ginger vampires stole everything not nailed down and loaded heaps of gold and booze into their Tesla Model X. This particular Tesla was painted blood red and modified to include a blood bar in the trunk. Musk also included a free hydraulic folding mechanism that raised the blood bar up and down as a gift for killing off his rival Marcus 'squealy' Zuckerstein. The blood bar's mechanism activated with the push of a red miniature bat skull button.

The gingers drove to Sex in Satan's Chair

nightclub at the corner of Bourbon and St.

Louis Street. The valet Morticia Gambino

greeted them and said, "Good evening,

ladies, its ladies' night and only hot fang

bitches drink free. The ugly methed-up

ones pay double the money since they do

not have any teeth. Will this be a business

or pleasure affair this evening?" Melanie

said, "Why not both? Here are five gold

coins to piss off and keep the change you

filthy animal!" The gingers laughed and

walked inside the beautiful red velvet

adorned club. The valet Morticia rolled

her eyes and stroked her black hair. She

carefully parked the Tesla Model X, so her

picture did not end up on a milk carton

like in the 80s.

Mary approached the DJ booth and asked

Dust Master Flex (Dustin) to change the

song to Work Bitch by Britney Spears.

Dust Master Flex was higher than Christ

from the acid he dropped, and he happily

obliged. The gingers danced and made out

with all the women in the nightclub which

angered the human cuckold men that were

hoping to score pussy that night. Melanie

walked up to a cute goth babe with blue

and black hair to suck her tongue. The

goth babe's husband did not like that, and

he tried to pull the ginger off his wife.

Melanie grabbed his balls and squeezed

the family jewels very hard. The human

man winced in pain and said, "Fine

vampire lady, you can have my hot wife I

am done with her cheating ass anyways."

As he walked away Melanie grabbed him

by the throat, kicked him in the stomach

and dragged him to the bathroom to drink

his blood. She dazed him with blue

voodoo dust so he would forget her face.

Melanie grabbed his wallet, stole his credit

card, and bought the cute goth babe drinks

all night on his coin.

Melanie said to her sisters and the goth

babe, "We must have sex in Satan's Chair

tonight!" Satan's Chair was very tall and

made from red velvet. It had a human

skull on each end of the back of the chair.

Margaret said, "Agreed! It has been two

weeks since I had been pleasured in

Satan's Chair. It is one of my favorite

places to fuck in like a drunken prom

queen. I need to soak the seat cushion in

my sweet lady juices!" Mary chimed in

and said, "How delightful that I get to

have my honey pot plowed by a big

hungry dick!" After we take turns getting

fucked in the chair, we get to extort the

poor bloke who owns this joint!"

The gingers headed to the basement of the night club and called upon Agent 0069 Sam Jordan and her part time boyfriend Steven Myers to join the fun. The chair had black wrist straps for bondage action and a vibrating vagina tickler and penetrator for the women that could be powered on by praying to the Devil.

A satanic cult meeting was taking place in an adjacent room. Edmond Brennan, a human warlock, were having their black

mass and he read passages from the

Satanic Bible written by Lavey. Edmond

was the leader of the cult and his followers

chanted "Hail Satan" after every verse was

spoken. The chants were loud enough for a

Catholic Priest to hear from outside.

The Catholic Priest heard the chanting and

made a sign of the cross since the chants

frightened him. The priest was sad that

these degenerates were worshipping the

Adversary instead of the Lord, Jesus Christ. The priest prayed five Our Father's and five Hail Mary's in an attempt to redirect his fearful thoughts into positive Christ like ones.

A Deadly Switcher approached the priest and said, "Suppose your night sucks listening to scary Satanic chants tonight on Bourbon street. Your night is about to get a whole lot worse after I suck the Jesus blood out of your veins. I am about to kill

you priest and drain your balls dry. Not
necessarily in that order."

The priest pulled out his .357 magnum
equipped with silver bullets and stuck it in
the gender-bender's mouth and educated
it. The man of God said to it, "Deadly
Switcher! I send you to hell in the name of
the Father, Son, and Holy Ghost. There
you will be tortured by demons and beaten
by the nine princes of hell for all eternity!"
The priest pulled the trigger and sent a

shockwave through the Deadly Switcher's

skull, spraying its brains all over Bourbon

street. After the priest sprayed the

sidewalk red with brain, bone, hair, and

blood, the priest pissed on its corpse. The

priest hopped in his beautiful blue 2022

Corvette Stingray and drove off into the

night.

Lord Alexander slipped passed the gingers

and took three beautiful blonde women

and began fucking them in Satan's chair.

Mary yelled, "This is not fair Lord
Alexander we were here first, and we
should be fucking in Satan's Chair! We
were not aware you would be in this club
tonight. We thought you would still be
fucking the Mad Doctor to kingdom
come."

Lord Alexander replied, "Fuck that
goddamn Mad Doctor bitch. Gingers these
are sexy nurses. Sexy nurses these are
gingers. That is the spot naked nurse
Nancy! Make the King of New Orleans

harder than iron wood and swallow all my unholy white load!" The nurses giggled after the mafia don said that and the gingers rolled their eyes in frustration.

Lord Alexander told the gingers, "Come here gingers and swallow the King's royal milk!" The King banged all the women in the night club and throat fucked them until they all had multiple orgasms and the women shook like a one-legged hooker on valium. The women inside the night club were exhausted and satisfied. They wore

the King's milk on their faces and

beautiful breasts as a slutty badge of

honor.

The gingers left Satan's Chair and went

looking for the club owner Jerry

Richardson. Jerry was easy to spot since

he was an eight-foot-tall vampire that

looked and dressed exactly like Jesus.

Jerry wore a creamy white colored linen

tunic and pranced around the night club

pretending to be the Christ. Vampire

Jesus' perm and beard was perfect and

always on point.

The gingers approached him upstairs in his

office and shook him down with guns to

get Vampire Jesus to pay back the illegally

high interest loan the King gave him a

month ago. Mary and Margaret held

Vampire Jesus by the throat and up against

the wall with the heels of their leather

boots. Jerry stuck his hands in tunics

pockets and grabbed five hundred gold

coins. He stretched his hands out like

Jesus and handed the gold over to the

gingers.

After the hot gingers robbed Vampire

Jesus, they took him downstairs and

fucked him in Satan's Chair. Vampire

Jesus had no balls figuratively speaking

and handed the gingers more vampire gold

since they damn near fucked him into a

coma. Melanie said, "Thank you Vampire

Jesus for the extra gold coins! We will

throw in an extra month of protection from

the angels this month free of charge. Enjoy

not being able to walk for a week after my

sisters and I fucked your brains out."

Vampire Jesus waved goodbye, and you

could see the scars on the inside of his

palms since he was the criminal crucified

two thousand years ago with the real

Jesus. Vampire Jesus fell asleep after the

gingers left and passed out with three

strippers and a Warsteiner beer in his left

hand.

The gingers finished their loan shark

collections from other night clubs and

went back to Sex in Satan's Chair night

club. They strutted around like they owned

the place. The ginger vampires drank

blood from the patrons and strippers

without killing anyone this time. On the

other hand, Lord Alexander sat nude in

Satan's Chair with the Mad Doctor riding him like Seabiscuit.

Lord Alexander and the Mad Doctor drank blood out of solid gold goblets and fucked at the same time. They pleasure each other and the Mad Doctor asked why the red velvet throne was called Satan's Chair. Lord Alexander told the Mad Doctor the reason it is called Satan's Chair is because it belongs to the Devil himself.

The legend goes that Satan took a vacation

from hell and carried his throne with him

on top of his Porsche Cayenne Turbo S.

He drove down Bourbon street higher than

six nuns on PCP and stumbled into the

night club when it was called Fleurty Girl.

He went to the basement and slept with

everyone inside the club on top of one of

his thrones. Satan became white girl

wasted and forgot where he was at after

the orgy. He drunkenly stumbled to his

Porsche Cayenne and forgot his favorite

chair and Satan returned to retrieve it.

Vampire Jesus inherited the club from his uncle Vinny and inherited his estate. Jerry saw Satan's Chair and renamed the club to Sex in Satan's Chair to honor the greatest orgy ever on Bourbon Street. Satan and Vampire Jesus banged three city blocks full of people that night. Vampire Jesus made a fortune after renaming the club and Lord Alexander capitalized on this massive revenue shortly after the name change. Satan told Vampire Jesus, "Hey you, Jesus-looking mother fucker, why

don't you have sex with this raven-haired,

blue eyed whore in Satan's Chair?"

Vampire Jesus and the Devil play cards

every Tuesday evening when Satan gets

stupidly drunk and forgets he is the ruler

of hell.

All clubs in New Orleans must pay bribes

and kickbacks to Lord Alexander since he

offers protection from the feds and the

local cops. All the human and vampire

clubs in New Orleans evade their taxes and are falsely listed as Catholic charities on their IRS tax forms. Lord Alexander keeps the monkey off the club owners backs since the feds will not come near him or his vampire crime business since his power is worldwide and he is protected by the Vampire God. Lord Alexander's vampire mafia protects all clubs from being federally investigated for crimes including racketeering, murder, extortion, drug dealing, tax evasion, prostitution, illegal gambling, and loansharking.

Lord Alexander got up from Satan's Chair and decided it was a great idea to smoke more Past, Present, and Future weed. Lord Alexander summoned Big Gay Salazar with his phone and said, "Hey, fat bastard, the King of New Orleans needs to get higher than Christ from your fortune teller weed!" Big Gay Salazar replied, "I cannot bring you weed I am about to bang my lovers in my big scary bed. I found a young twenty-two-year-old man and convinced him to leave his wife for me. I

cannot get you stoned tonight my King."

Lord Alexander quickly threatened Big

Gay Salazar and said, "Listen, you fat

gypsy motherfucker, you. You only exist

in this city because of me. Without my

protection, you personally, would be

passed around by every werewolf cartel

member and would be forced to turn sex

tricks for them. Then where are you going

to go? Back to Montana? Fuck Montana,

fuck your 'boyfriend' and fuck you. You will bring me that Past, Present, and Future weed, or I will have three vampire wise guys forcibly take it from your fat gypsy hands. These wise guys have been begging me to give the signal to have your fat fortune teller ass thrown into the Gulf of Mexico weighted down with dumbbells. Do not show up with your gay lover either. Another thing in this city I rule everyone and everything. Every vampire wise guy answer to me and do not forget that."

Big Gay Salazar spilled his coffee all over himself and hung up the phone with the King. He was nervous since he knew the King was notorious for having anyone brutally murdered for disobeying his orders. A fate which Big Gay Salazar's racketeering best friend Harley Puccio from the New York City Bianchi Family met a year ago.

Big Gay Salazar showed up to Sex in Satan's Chair nightclub and brought his young lovers anyway. He got too stoned off his other strain Devil's Tail and forgot that he was not supposed to brink Kirk or Ralph. The five gingers appeared behind Big Gay Salazar out of thin air and re-instructed the fat bastard. Melanie told him, "You were under strict orders not to bring that little faggot here. I do not care if Vampire Jesus loves the little faggots. We do not. You are only tolerated because the King likes the drugs you smoke. Suppose

Lord Alexander, found out you brought that little booty hole pirate here! You, him, and your back door psychiatrist Ralph would be executed in the desert."

Lord Alexander showed up and saw that Big Gay Salazar brought his two lovers of the faggot persuasion with him to the club. He ordered Big Gay Salazar beat up and his two lovers to be executed outside the club. Lord Alexander let his fortune teller friend live since his weed was stronger than anyone else and Big Gay Salazar kept the secret on how to grow the magical pot.

Three burly vampire wise guys showed up and stuffed Kirk and Ralph into a blacked-out van and shot them both in the back of the head with .22 caliber pistols. The gangster terrorists drank their blood and threw their lifeless bodies in the Gulf of Mexico as ordered by Lord Alexander, never to be seen again. That was power you cannot buy.

The King gave Big Gay Salazar a hand towel and told him to clean himself up and wipe the blood off the floor. Big Gay Salazar cleaned up his own blood and cried silently as the vampire gangsters mocked him. He pulled out his rainbow bong and tried to hand it to Lord Alexander. Lord Alexander kicked it out of his hand and said, "This is not time for your pride to show. Bring out your red glass bong with the vampire bats or get your ass whipped by Fat Tommy again.

The rainbow bong shattered on the floor

and Big Gay Salazar swept it up and put it

in his rainbow purse since he did not want

to anger the King anymore.

Big Gay Salazar smoked out the King and

the five gingers with his Past, Present, and

Future weed. He sent the six vampire

gangsters and himself two hundred years

into the future with his time-bending

fortune teller weed. In the future peace

was prevalent throughout the earth. The world's citizens celebrated the banishment of the god of everything every year during Mardi Gras season. Humanity celebrated by getting drunker than three circus clowns and orgies were widespread. Humanity's population tripled since the year 2025. Lord Alexander and the gingers observed a lone vampire god of the earth in the distance but could not make out who it was supposed to be.

Lord Alexander and his gangster whores smoked another bowl of the fortune teller weed and saw that Lord Vincent was being held captive in an interdimensional prison in the past. The King told Big Gay Salazar that he saw enough of the future and was satisfied. Lord Alexander the vampire don told Big Gay Salazar to transport them back in time so they could rescue Lord Vincent from Ka-Ching and his demon cartel.

The King landed back in the Sex in

Satan's Chair nightclub and telepathically

told the leader of ORACLE, Tamara of

Lord Vincent's current location and that

he needs rescued from Ka-Ching. Tamara

showed up dressed to the nines with her

digitally computerized tactical gear that

made her invisible to everyone inside the

club. Tamara met privately with the King

in Vampire Jesus' office and told him

what the acronym ORACLE that night. It

is Orleans Raven-hearted Ass-kicking

Clandestine Lethal Empaths. The secretive

and elite vampire intelligence organization formed by Tamara and Domino under direct orders from Lord Vincent thousands of years ago. The empath portion of the acronym is from the Vampire God training them so hard that it honed their emotion sensing skills. The ORACLE vampires were all gifted the ability to sense and read the emotions of others from far greater distance than a normal vampire.

The ORACLE organization is an elite all black vampire unit that is special forces capable. Theses ORACLE immortals are the best bad ass intelligence gathering, crime fighting, war mongering vampires on the planet. Their training is so secretive that only Lord Vincent knows about it. Their marksmanship, intelligence, and hand-to-hand combat skills are a true force to be reckoned with throughout the universe. The only vampire known to beat them in all aspects of combat is the Vampire God Vincent. Nobody holds a

candle stick to these lethal Black vampire
women.

All supernatural creatures including angels
and demons tremble at the sight of these
special forces' women. They tremble in
fear if the ORACLE shows up because
they know they are about to meet their
maker in the afterlife. The ORACLE
immortals were exceptional at killing their
targets in complete silence and that is why
they were feared by everyone. No remorse

when they killed their target, it was only business as usual and never personal.

Although they have been around since Ancient Egypt their existence was only recently revealed to Lord Alexander by Lord Vincent on a need-to-know basis. Lord Alexander was one of three members from the vampire mafia council to know that the ORACLE existed.

Lord Alexander and Tamara conversed about Ka-Ching holding Lord Vincent captive in his Temple of Sex and Pain. Tamara already knew Lord Vincent was being held in the interdimensional prison thanks to a half-demon confidential informant named Joey 'Two Shot' Beluccio. The King said to Tamara, "You are the elite ORACLE! What must we do to bring back Lord Vincent, so he does not meet a similar fate like the god of darkness? I will have to kill Ka-Ching for this treachery. He will longer count coin long time, ever again!"

Tamara told the King that their private clandestine plane was currently being fueled with Satan Fire Juice and they would all leave soon. Tamara and Domino handed the King, five gingers and the Mad Doctor, demon buster guns lined with chaos energy bullets. The ORACLE also outfitted them the same tactical gear they were wearing. An invisible, digitally cloaked plane awaited them at the New

Orleans International Airport.

The ORACLE's private plane was

powered by solar and moonlight energy

and used zero fossil fuels. It was flown by

a voice activated artificially intelligent

super learning computer, named Arnie.

The special aircraft had its own mind and

could think and speak independently from

Tamara or Domino.

THE LOVERS CARD

Vampire Jesus also known as Bourbon

Jesus was known for performing miracles

with his dragon bone wand. He turned

water into bourbon with this wand he

always carried with him in his Versace

satchel. Bourbon Jesus would get drunk on fairy and dwarf blood and begin preaching to his night club members. He would hypnotize the patrons of his bar and entice people to leave half of their paychecks as tips, since he collected a percentage from the bartenders. Vampire Jesus would lie to the drunkards under hypnosis and convince them he was really Jesus and had multiple children to feed.

Bourbon Jesus would preach his fifty

percent donation nonsense and bang every

mans wife while he sat on Satan's Chair.

His favorite wife to bang was Mrs.

Falcone, who was Italian werewolf

mobster Jimmy 'The baby arm' Falcone's

wife. Jimmy was always out of town doing

the 'family business' and was hardly

around to keep track of Mrs. Falcone.

Suppose Jimmy 'the baby arm' caught the

two doing sex, the two lovers would be

gunned down inside Sex In Satan's Chair

night club and stuffed in an oil barrel by

the end of the week. Vampire Jesus was under Lord Alexander's protection and that meant he was untouchable to any werewolf wise guy.

Vampire Jesus lecherous ways of life was another reason Lord Alexander made him pay higher kick backs to the racketeering kingpin. A werewolf wise guy by the name of Bobby 'the chin' Johnson was known to frequent the nightclub ran by Vampire Jesus.

Bobby 'the chin' was a close associate of the King of New Orleans. Bobby ran his own protection racket against Vampire Jesus with Lord Alexander's permission. Bobby knew Vampire Jesus was secretly bisexual and threatened to expose his secret to the world which would have gotten him murdered by Lord Alexander. No wise guy or associate is allowed to be gay or bisexual unless they are female. That rule was first made by the original

Vampire God Vincent since the dawn of man.

Although Bobby 'the chin' was werewolf he was actually the underboss to the Esplanade Vampire Crime Family and a capo in the Werewolf Mafia. Bobby was a big earner for the vampires since he knew how to cook ledger books and make their business dealings harder to track by the feds. Bobby 'the chin' got that nickname since he had a cleft chin and was incredibly handsome.

The King would get drunk from consuming too much dwarf blood and rum and would misdial Bobby 'the chin' occasionally. He would randomly call Bobby at two in the morning and say good morning beautiful thinking it was his wife the Mad Doctor. The two friends would laugh about the mistake when Lord Alexander was stone cold sober.

Bobby 'the chin' also ran his prostitution racket inside the Sex in Satan's chair night club. Basically, he would help Vampire Jesus give the patrons an ungodly amount of cheap booze. The pair would lure men and women into having sex with prostitutes who were keen on cleaning out the patrons' wallets after they fucked them into a coma.

Bobby 'the chin' was underboss so

Vampire Jesus had no choice but to let

Bobby take the larger percentage of the

prostitution racket. Lord Alexander told

Vampire Jesus that should he complain

about the way the family did business,

then he should start his own family.

Vampire Jesus knew that meant he had to

shut the fuck up and bite the bullet so to

speak. Suppose he decided to run his own

family, which meant he would have to

leave New Orleans. Bourbon Jesus knew

every immortal wise guy from Chicago to

LA would take an even larger cut than the King of New Orleans.

Bobby 'the chin' went to the New Orleans Voodoo School for interesting children before he was turned into a werewolf. He used his knowledge of voodoo to put roots on Satan's Chair. It made the chair entice humans to pleasure themselves and stay at the club way longer than they intended to do. This was a ruse to get people to invite all their wealthy friends and spend more gold than they intended to spend.

Bobby 'the chin' never paid for his drinks at Sex in Satan's Chair nightclub since Vampire Jesus was beneath him in the hierarchy of the family. Vampire Jesus had to shell out the extra cost and put the extravagant amount on his own credit card. He knew better than to complain because Bobby 'the chin' beat him up on several occasions in the past.

Another way Bobby 'the chin' was smart

was he always invested his massive

earnings and rarely spent his own money.

It was always someone else that had to

foot his bill since he was the underboss

and had the power to have people

executed without going to a council of

nine or King's solo vote. Bobby the 'the

chin' was about eighty percent straight and

twenty percent bisexual man when drunk.

Since he was werewolf the decree Lord

Vinent made did not apply to him and he was permitted to be a switch hitter since he made 'the family' a fortune.

Bobby 'the chin' left the club and met up with Big Gay Salazar since he was the only gypsy in New Orleans who knew how to grow Past, Present, Future weed. Bobby paid two vampire gold coins to hit the fortune tellers weed and another five coins to have his fortune read. Big Gay Salazar showed him two different futures which involved him making an important

loyalty decision. It was either marry his

high school crush Suzie Martinez or

Princess Tiffanie.

If he married Suzie Martinez, the King

would give him a twenty percent pay raise

and an extra vacation since being in the

mob had its perks. Suppose he married

Princess Tiffanie instead his future would

be dire, and he would be sold into sex

slavery in Mexico never to be heard from

again. Bobby knew that Suzie was the better choice and decided that was the real future. He was not stupid and knew better than to double cross the boss of the family.

Big Gay Salazar gave Bobby 'the chin' free fortune teller weed, and Bobby would sit on his lap like a little back door bitch. Bobby would join both women and men every Sunday morning for a weekly fuck fest right on Jackson Square in front of St. Louis Cathedral and they would mock the

Catholic religion for not keeping up with

the times.

The King loathed anyone that was not

straight and hired werewolves to beat up

people from the rainbow community. Lord

Alexander also made the wolves wash his

Porsche three times a week and paid them

a paltry wage too. They did this out of fear

and respect since the vampire mafia had a

council of nine that ruled the world under

Lord Vincent.

Big Gay Salazar pulled out his crystal ball

and beckoned Lord Alexander to sit at his

table in Jackson Square. He read the

King's future and said although the Mad

Doctor would betray him soon, she would

be married to him until the end of time.

When pressed about the betrayal, Big Gay

Salazar told Lord Alexander, the Mad

Doctor would be flipped into turning

against the King by her ugly best friend

Jasmine, who was the leader of the vampire cartel based out of Mexico.

The King of New Orleans believe he would be married to the Mad Doctor after pulling the Lover's Card in three separate future readings. He did not understand why his wife would betray him and be flipped into a Mexican Drug Cartel. Lord Alexander cheated on the Mad Doctor, but it was forbidden for her to do the same.

Lord Alexander enjoyed his whoremongering throughout New Orleans and Mexico. The King went to Mexico on a road trip and turned a gorgeous math teacher named Sophia Gomez into a vampire and secret lover. This love affair was discovered by the Mad Doctor since she and Jasmine had the King followed there by a group of werewolf cartel members that worked directly for Jasmine. This would eventually cost the King something precious but that would not come until later. Lord Alexander was a modern-day immortal Casanova, and he was careless when it came to hiding his secret lovers from his wife.

Lord Alexander's favorite mistress was the math teacher. Sophia Gomez was twenty-six and the most gorgeous Mexican woman he ever laid eyes upon. He was so smitten with her beauty that his long hard cock made his brain fall in love with this bodacious babe. The Mad Doctor was so jealous of this gorgeous newly turned vampire that she plotted with

Jasmine to have them both kidnapped and

murdered by the Mexican Werewolf

Cartel.

The god of everything manipulated the

King's relationships with her mind-

bending-power. Zarah was jealous that

Lord Alexander was spreading his potent

immortal seed all over god's creation. The

Mad Doctor secretly cheated on the King

of New Orleans with ten black and

bearded, demonic dwarves since she knew

the King was a wee bit racist and was

payback for the Sophia Gomez affair.

THE DEADLY SWITCHERS

OVERTAKE NEW ORLEANS

Zarah summoned Princess Tiffanie and Ka-Ching to one of her secret hideouts called Stilettos Strip Club on Bourbon street where she held her second job. They discussed overtaking New Orleans from the vampire mafia and killing their King. Zarah and the Deadly Switchers unleashed a surprise attack against the city of New

Orleans for Zarah's amusement.

Since Ka-Ching was now in New Orleans

that meant the ORACLE would reach the

Temple of Sex and Pain since the dwelling

was more vulnerable without Ka-Ching.

Lord Vincent sensed there was hope for

his old dusty bones. Lord Vincent and

George, the cat, no longer feared death,

but embraced their ORACLE savior to

rescue them from the interdimensional prison.

Zarah resurrected Yogi Jimi from death since he was beastly when it came to combat skills. Since Zarah was the god of everything, she could have simply wiped the whole city off the map with just a thought. Instead, she chose a traditional war against New Orleans because it brought her laughter and entertainment. Zarah knew nobody would defeat her since her physical body and divinity outranked anything known to universe.

One of the only ways Zarah could get off sexually was to watch the Vampire Mafia and the Deadly Switchers kill each other off with extreme violence. War and chaos were invented by Zarah to keep the universe from getting overpopulated. Zarah grew tired of depopulating entire planets herself and would incite wars to watch the worlds burn.

Zarah gave Princess Tiffanie and Ka-Ching, deadly weapons to pass out to the Deadly Switchers and demon gangs that worked for Ka-Ching. These battle weapons were Zarah powered swords, rainbow guns to kill vampires and make humans transgender, and Haitian voodoo death wands that were a one shot kill.

The mafia vampire and his immortal friends knew this war would be a fight for the entire universe as the unstable god of

everything would wipe all existence with

just a thought. Lord Alexander knew that

Zarah was psychologically unstable and a

danger to herself and all life on earth.

Zarah blamed her creation for her failure

to design the perfect universe and was

unable to admit fault since she was

'perfect.'

A resurrected Yogi Jimi became

disillusioned with Zarah and her plans to

undo her creation. He decided that he liked

the Vampire God Vincent and saw him as

a friend and student. Yogi Jimi was a man

of honor and integrity. Yogi Jimi left New

Orleans in search of Lord Vincent inside

the Temple of Sex and Pain.

Yogi Jimi knew the layout of the desert

temple and knew precisely how to defeat

the interdimensional demon babes who

tortured Lord Vincent and his talking

feline best friend. Yogi Jimi trained under the original

Buddha and Buddha helped him hone his combat skills to become a great warrior.

The Deadly Switcher terrorists bombed the whole city of New Orleans with aircraft stolen from the United States Airforce. Large and small explosions erupted everywhere and there was nowhere to run or hide. Tens of thousands of innocent civilians were killed in the surprise attack. Princess Tiffanie, Ka-Ching, Zarah, and ten thousand Deadly Switchers descended upon the city from the skies and massacred thousands of homeless inhabitants living under the bridges.

Zarah said, "These immoral homeless people are stinking up the city with their tent cities and unwashed booty holes. We must eradicate these villainous people from the planet and cleanse them from society." Zarah had no remorse as she savagely decapitated a hundred homeless citizens in the blink of an eye.

The Deadly Switchers flew Boeing B-29 Superfortress planes near the Esplanade Mansion and tried to destroy Lord Alexander's home. Dawn Lightfoot, 0069 Sam Jordan, and The Great Lou stopped them with powerful voodoo magic. The trio sealed the building making it impervious to any physical attack and this angered Zarah and her Deadly Switcher underlings.

The Elite Daytime Guardians took out the bombers with AT4 rocket launchers and called in an artillery strike to take out one of the Deadly Switcher camps found across the street at City Park. The Elite Daytime Guardians and two hundred gangster vampires grabbed sniper rifles and killed three hundred gender-bending vampires from the rooftop. Kreaper oversaw the rooftop assault, and he

ordered both the vampire and human

snipers to spread out and cover all sides of

the Esplanade Mansion.

Kreaper said, "Show no mercy to those

android gender-bender vampire scum.

Aim for the heart or head. Lord Alexander

supplied us with enough weaponry to hold

them off until he returns with Lord

Vincent. Buckle up buttercups! This is not

Afghanistan or Somalia. These Deadly

Switchers are far more agile and vigorous in combat compared to the human terrorist villagers we slaughtered in war."

The Great Lou, 0069 Sam Jordan, and Dawn Lightfoot grabbed scoped, and laser sighted, M4 service rifles, borrowed from the United States Marine Corps, and began firing upon the Deadly Switchers on Moss street and then City Park Avenue. Wizards, warlocks, and sorcerers were known to multi-class with firearms in case

they got too high and ran out of magic
spells.

The Deadly Switchers did not retreat since
Zarah blessed them and took away their
fear of death. The rainbow vampires tried
to repel the relentless assault with their
AK-47s but were not successful since the
guns were not as accurate as the M4.
Princess Tiffanie beat ten humans and five
wizards to death with its massive horse leg
that hung out of its skirt. Princess Tiffanie

laughed maniacally after she decapitated the humans with her sword. It snorted fruity flavored rainbow meth to boost its energy and speed to maximum level.

Ka-Ching landed on the rooftop of the Esplanade Mansion and said to the Vampire Mafia, "Me love you long time. Here are six few grenades to wish you happy birthday and good night, Irene. Lord Alexander is a fool if he thinks we cannot take this city in his absence. He will fail trying to rescue Lord Vincent

from the Temple of Sex and Pain."

Bobby 'the chin' Johnson shot Ka-Ching

in his right shoulder and said, "You may

be a treacherous flea bag from Beijing and

a terrible accountant, but we are Chicago!"

A hundred vampires from the Chicago

outfit showed up on the rooftop which

caused Ka-Ching to flee in terror. The

Chicago vampire gangster outfit was

armed with M27 Infantry Automatic

Rifles stolen from the Camp Lejune,

Marine Corps Infantry training base. They

shot at Ka-Ching, and he leaped from the

rooftop just in time and flew to St. Charles

Avenue. Bobby 'the chin' called 'Broke

Back' Biden on the phone to send in the

Marine Corps Recon Marines and Army

Delta Force special forces for

reinforcements. 'Brokeback' Biden

refused to send in the elite units since he

was cowardly and not a real leader.

'Brokeback' Biden was in a highly

classified sexual relationship with Princess Tiffanie.

The King's demon dwarves threw explosive red fireball bombs from the rooftop of the Esplanade Mansion hitting the Deadly Swithers' faces to slow them down. The Deadly Switchers retreated down Esplanade Avenue since the dwarves bombarded them and cost them their position.

Kreaper called upon Don 'Rocky' Gambino of the elite St. Claude werewolf family and explained the grave situation at hand. Don Gambino ordered half of his werewolf capos and lieutenants to reinforce the Esplanade Mansion and City Park strategic position. The other half went downtown to the French Quarter to help fend off the full-scale invasion. The werewolf gangsters were competent marksmen trained by Marine Corps Recon snipers during the second invasion of Iraq. This werewolf training operation was top-secret that only Bush and Cheney knew about.

Zarah, Princess Tiffanie, and Ka-Ching flew around the city terrorizing civilians and unleashing hell upon New Orleans. Zarah, the god of everything, ordered the two vampires to shoot, eat, and kill the little children hiding in their schools.

Princess Tiffanie and Ka-Ching used their guns and death wands to massacre an entire elementary school. Three hundred students were slaughtered in the blink of an eye and the vampires gorged the blood from their little corpses. This onslaught happened so fast that Kreaper was unable to rescue them, and he cried out in pain at the horror he saw.

Kreaper called Lord Alexander on his Kryptall iPhone and said, "My King you need to hurry the fuck up and get back to New Orleans! Our forces are overwhelmed with Zarah's, and we might

not make it to next week." Lord Alexander

replied, "Do not retreat, Kreaper! Attack

them from a different position. Call my

friends from Los Angeles they can get

there within an hour. The LA Shark Tooth

gang is some of the most violent

motherfuckers you ever met. They have

more weaponry than god and are fearless

like you. You will be in charge of

overseeing the entire defense of New

Orleans since you have the most combat

experience."

The King of New Orleans and his wife the Mad Doctor aborted their mission in rescuing the Vampire God, since they knew the ORACLE was capable of handling that mission without them.

Lord Alexander and the Mad Doctor showed up and listened to the resurrected Princess Tiffanie call them out from the shadows. Princess Tiffanie said, "Come on out King and Queen and fight me like the ravenous boner killers you are tonight.

Princess Tiffanie waited for them riding her dragon in a dark alley on St. Ann street.

The King and the Mad Doctor showed up and released their own furious repel and assault against the Deadly Switchers. They were equipped with high classified assault rifles designed by Sir-Tweets-A lot. The rifles were artificially super-intelligent guns that were programmed to aim for the head or heart of the Deadly Switchers. The rifles only needed to be pointed in the general direction of a rainbow vampire and fired without input from the user.

The King and Mad Doctor slaughtered three thousand Deadly Switchers in retaliation for the school massacre that took place moments before they arrived. The Mad Doctor saw Princess Tiffanie strangling a young female college student and intervened. The Mad Doctor violently ripped Princess Tiffanie off the student and stabbed her in the back with a silver combat knife. The Mad Doctor yelled, "Here is your last supper, sup on this bitch!" Princess Tiffanie winced and gasped in pain and let the young woman go, then fled the alley on her rainbow dragon.

The city appeared gruesome as dead bodies piled up in the streets and sidewalks. Deadly Switchers descended upon the inhabitants of New Orleans and killed a third of the city. People screamed

in terror as their throats were slit and

blood drained by the gender-bending

vampires. Zarah cackled like the wicked

witch of the southwest as the screams

were music to her ancient ears.

Lord Alexander and the Mad Doctor took

to the skies and flew over to Esplanade

Avenue and were greeted by three

Catholic Priests. The trio's leader was

Father John and he said to the King, "Lord

Alexander, Zarah's unholy army is destroying our beautiful city. Over half of the buildings downtown have been blown to smithereens. We must pray to the true God, our Lord Jesus Christ and St. Michael for protection from these monsters."

Lord Alexander saw no harm in this priest's faith, and they prayed with him. The Mad Doctor left her husband and the priests to give orders to the gingers and

Elite Daytime Guardians. The Great Lou and 0069 Sam Jordan were on top of the roof of the Esplanade Mansion fighting their hearts out with the Elite Daytime Guardians.

The Mad Doctor and five gingers traveled underground in tunnels to escape the carnage and regroup in case the voodoo protection spell by Dawn Lightfoot failed. 0069 Sam Jordan and the Great Lou went into a warrior trance and frenzy. They killed dozens of Deadly Switchers with their chaos magic staffs. They blasted an ungodly amount of energy and disintegrated the gender-bender enemies, which enraged Zarah tenfold.

Lord Alexander teamed up with the Catholic Priests and, repelling several Deadly Switchers with an ungodly amount of firepower. They fired and outmaneuvered Zarah's Army and repelled them away from Esplanade Mansion. The vampire and priests drove them to a choke point in the French Quarter where they were able to kill another thousand Deadly Switchers.

Zarah spoke out from the sky and said, "Lord Alexander this battle is just the beginning sweetheart. I am just getting warmed up. How do you feel about warm weather?" Zarah outstretched her left hand and raised the air temperature with her mind to one-hundred-and-thirty-degrees

Fahrenheit. The vampires did not mind the increase, but the humans complained of the air being hotter than Satan's ball sack.

Lord Alexander gave the priests swords in case they ran out of Pope Francis blessed ammunition. Father John said, "This is the most violent I have ever seen in New Orleans and is the darkest night so far this year. We must kill off these gender-bending vampires and Zarah before this marvelous city burns to the ground. Here is an extra crucifix and St. Michael

pendant blessed by the Pope himself.

Wear these to protect your soul from evil."

Lord Alexander said, "So, priest, St.

Michael is real after all? I am dying to

meet him because he was my favorite

angel from the Bible before I became this

ten-foot vampire mafia monster boss you

see with your eyes." The priest replied,

"St. Michael cannot be here to help as he

is busy fighting the devil to prevent him

from escaping hell. Zarah is not the god of everything, but she is the Anti-Christ foretold by the book of Revelation. Zarah is a result of the real God punishing the world for living in sin for thousands of years. Jesus will come to defeat her I promise."

The King of New Orleans was highly skeptical of the priest's belief that Zarah was not the god of everything. The priest's beliefs were irrelevant at this point since saving the city was the King's number one

priority. The last bit of Lord Alexander's

silver aura flashed brightly, and it became

solid gold like Lord Vincent's. During the

transformation to one hundred percent

potent vampire god a Deadly Switcher

attacked the priests and one tried to kill

Father John with a sword.

Lord Alexander's potential was fully

awakened, and he caught the sword with

his right index finger before it could kill

his priest friend. Lord Alexander forgot all fear and anxiety and focused wholly on winning the war. He emptied his thoughts and shoved his left middle finger into the eye socket of the Deadly Switcher, killing it instantly. He said to the priest, "Father John, my fully awakened vampire god power, is power you cannot buy from Costco." The priests and Lord Alexander laughed, and the Deadly Switchers rainbow corpse fell to the earth. There was blood and brain everywhere.

Made in the USA
Columbia, SC
07 September 2023

f2223031-40de-4274-8944-6695f409d4e1R01